THE FIRST MATE OF NEMAIN'S REVENGE

THE FIRST MATE OF NEMAIN'S REVENGE

PREQUEL NOVELLA

NEMAIN'S REVENGE
BOOK 0.5

MCKENZIE A HATTON

PRONUNCIATION GUIDE FOR MAP

Samsara: sam-SAHraw
Kheli: KHEE-lih
Carriwitchet: karr-e-wIHtch-eht
Brettania: brit-AY-ni-ah
Koi No Yokan: koy-noh-YOE-khahn
Draiocht: drah-ou-SHET
Keraunos: kAIRa-ounohs
Toska: TUH-skah
Sumerian: suh-mAIR-ian

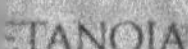

ETANOIA
SUMERIAN SEA
NERII
CASCADES
ATLAS
DEAD MAN'S
WASTES
QUARAFA
RUINS OF
OLD KALON
SAMSARA
CARRIWITCHET
ISLES

TOSKA
BREVIS
BRETTANIA
PYRIA
LUCIS
KOI NO
YOKAN
DRAIOCHT
KHELI
KERAUNOS SEA

MCKENZIE A HATTON

Copyright © 2024 by McKenzie A Hatton

All rights reserved.

No part of this book may be reproduced in any form or by any electronic or mechanical means, including information storage and retrieval systems, without written permission from the author, except for the use of brief quotations in a book review.

Cover Design by Maria Spada (www.mariaspada.com)
Editing by Rachel Ohm (www.rachelo300.wixsite.com/website/work)
Scene Art by Hanna @sovana.art

 Created with Vellum

For those who've only known selfish bastards

PROLOGUE

A DESTINY OF DEATH

The dry air was rough on Captain Pike's skin, like the sand of this cursed place, drifting in the wind around him. After a fortnight traveling to the shore of Draiocht, with sand in unmentionable places, he hoped this would be worth his time.

He'd had years of the most successful piracy of his career, but then the dreams had come. They assaulted him with flashes of giants, sand, and the sea turning against him. *His* sea. He couldn't understand it, the sea was his to command, and the only master he answered to. How could She betray him?

Pike scratched at his accumulating beard. He'd once kept it cleanly shaven, but he was still unnerved by the new tattoo. Most of Nemain's 'gifts' were assets to his career. It struck fear into his enemies to see what he was capable of, but this one, it foretold of a fate he refused to believe. Every tattoo represented a list of debts he owed to the goddess. But this was different. The spell he had used to try to explain the dreams had only left him with this location and black stains on his face.

The place was as he dreamt it. A sandstone house in the middle of nowhere; Draiocht hieroglyphs painted in red across every inch of the structure's surface. Black curtains flapped in the wind, showing glimpses of the inside. Shelves of jars lined one wall with stacks of tools beside them. The middle of the structure housed a sandstone slab large enough for a human to lay across, red staining the center.

The vision told him not to enter the hovel, but to walk around it. Behind it was a bathtub, one made of stone with candles flickering in the sea breeze.

A head of inky black hair flowed over the side of the tub, but the woman heard his footsteps. She rose from the tub, and he witnessed her backside, a sight he would have admired otherwise had she not been covered in a thick layer of liquid obsidian that clung to her every curve. When she stepped out of the bathtub and faced him, he grew more concerned with the substance painting her. It was so dark that it allowed no shadow or light to penetrate its depths. He could not tell what her curves looked like other than her silhouette, despite her nakedness.

Only her head was spared, her golden skin making it obvious that she was no local, her skin all too light for her to be. Her eyes stole his attention. Milky white, like a necromite. Nemain's death walkers.

"Revenant of lost souls. You've finally arrived," she addressed, her voice smooth like fine rum.

"You were expecting me?"

"For decades."

He straightened, not liking the gravity in her gaze. "Then tell me what I dream. The sea betrays me, with storms, with creatures, with still sails and scorching suns. What does it mean?"

She approached slowly, the substance on her not sliding down her body in the slightest. When the witch was only a breath away from him, he could smell her. A scent fouler than weeks at sea. She smelled like her body was decaying.

"You deal in death, Captain Pike. Surely, you know its consequences."

His breath sharpened.

It was a side effect of the grimoire. One day, he would have to pay for the tattoos covering his skin. His lust for power was too great to stop the use of it.

"How could I not?"

"You seek the spell. The last spell you should ever need."

Immortality.

"That spell is a fool's hope. Only Nemain would be cruel enough to create a way to escape divine justice then make it impossible to enact. I've hunted for it. The blood of the cursed does not exist." She circled around him, a blackened hand trailing around him, but never touching his coat. Until she circled before him again, a card in hand.

A witch's tool of prediction.

The one she held was of a skeleton holding a freshly severed head. *Death.*

"Davina has already chosen your fate. There will be no escaping it." His stomach sank as if a cannon ball had been dropped inside him. Was that all Nemain wanted him to know? That his days were numbered.

"How long do I have?"

She laughed and the sound was light and airy, as pleasant as a siren. "Many years, but that will be precisely your problem."

Pike narrowed his eyes, stepping toward her and towering over her petite frame. "I don't have time for your games. How long?"

"Fifteen years." She smiled and it was too sharp. "The man who kills you will be the blood you need to live eternally."

Pike surged, his hands locking around her arms before she could flinch. The inky black liquid made her arms slippery, but he held on tight. "What cruel irony is this? Have you summoned me to mock me? Do. Not. Test me, witch."

"Temper," she cooed, mockery dripping from her airy tone. "You really shouldn't kill me until I've finished."

Reluctantly, he released her.

She turned from him, returning to the bath she had emerged from. "You will die, but may yet live forever."

He growled at her for not making sense, but the amusement on her face told him she enjoyed his frustration.

"Secure your blood and your legacy and you can have that chance."

It was his turn to laugh. "My legacy? I bed too many women to count. No doubt, I have dozens of children out there. My blood will survive."

She jumped, holding each side of the tub and hissing at him. He flinched backwards at the sight of her fangs. "Your pride will be the end of you, Captain Pike. And this time, I do not refer to your death." She glared at him, holding up one finger. "You have a single child left; all others have perished in the final war. I suggest you find her and breed her with someone who will make certain those children survive. If they do not, your death will be final." Swiping her hand in the air before her, his face tingled, then burned as short strands of hair fell from his chin to the sand below. "And your final form will only be the shell of a man."

Pike resisted the urge to lift his hands to his face where the barren inked skin depicted a necromite's mouth, agape and lips that had decayed enough to show teeth and bone.

"Build your legacy and die well, for Nemain is eager for your presence," she said, disappearing back into the light absorbing fluid, her face and hair vanishing into the eternal blackness.

Pike lunged for the tub, plunging his hand into the strange waters. "That can't be it. You haven't told me why. Why do I need grandchildren?" But his hand only swam in the liquid, feeling only the stone walls of the tub.

He growled again, standing and kicking over the tub. Finally, he recognized the fluid for what it was: necromite blood. He'd cleaned enough off his clothing and ship enough to know its strange properties. Like how it cleans from wood and cloth like oil, but it clings to skin like ink. He kicked over the tub. Dark liquid splashed out, pooling in the sand, but nothing emerged and his hand was stained with the blood of the dead.

CHAPTER I
BLOODY PIRATES

Metal clanged against metal as Joseph brought his hammer down on the newborn sword below him.

Smithing was in his blood. His father was a blacksmith and his father before him, it was all very mundane, but it was all he knew. His mother and father had died of cholera a few years back. All that was left of them was the blacksmith's hut.

The heat of the forge threatened to blister his hands as he worked.

Naval swords were all the same. A saber, quick and nimble, even if he had argued for the efficacy of longswords instead. The small colored tassel was the only difference that showed the rank of the officer. They all bore the Minister's seal pressed upon the steel, signifying their indentured service to the Minister and his Navy.

Joseph had seen so many of them, he'd lost count.

Truly, he preferred the long range a pistol provided over the close combat required for a sword. He often made those along with the swords for the Navy, but there were other shops crafting them. It was his swords he was known for. Although the blades he made were coveted, they paled in comparison to the masterpieces his father had made.

There was one sword he valued above all others, however. He could neither sell nor use it due to the Minister's ridiculous regulations. His father's prized sword hung on the wall, not used for anything more than decoration.

It was a magnificent piece, closer in design to a pirate's cutlass than an officer's saber, but it was beautiful. The curve of the steel, the heaviness of the handle that balanced out the weight of the blade. Any smith worth his salt would appreciate the craftsmanship. He'd been given offers to buy the blasted thing time and time again, but he had lacked the apathy to part with it. He had been surprised so many were willing to risk the Minister's wrath, had it been found in their possession.

Joseph's father had only managed to keep it as a personal decoration due to the Minister's gratitude for receiving the best sabers from his infamous skill. Joseph was the next best thing in the Minister's eyes. Still, Joseph often wondered how far that kindness would extend.

He fully expected the Minister to take it from him one day. At times, he wished he would. If that sword was gone, maybe he could finally move on with his life. Though in truth, that was an absurd notion. It wasn't only a sword that kept him glued to the blasted hut.

It was only easier to blame the piece of metal rather than his own reluctance to change.

Joseph shook off the thought, returning to pounding the heated steel below him.

Screams rang throughout the street outside. Joseph narrowed his eyes at the door, daring whatever monster was behind it to attack him while he was in a foul mood. The screams continued on, so he decided to investigate, leaving behind the work on his table.

He seized one of the sabers hanging from the rack at the corner of the room before heading to the door. He cursed, realizing he was not as skilled with the weapon as he would have liked, not finding ample opportunity to practice with the demand set forth by the Minister.

With this in mind, he strapped a pistol to his belt.

A billowing fire greeted Joseph as he exited his shop. Flames danced, lit with furniture and fabrics right in the center of the street, threatening to burn the buildings around it. The citizens of low town had gathered, bringing buckets of water from wells and the nearby sea to put the fire out. But around them—

Pirates.

They laughed while throwing more fuel on the fire and tossing people away from it. There was no way to stop the spread with them in the way.

Joseph tried not to think too hard about the thrill that ran through his blood as he faced a pirate, ducking away from the blade swinging towards him. It was a titanium cutlass, probably smuggled from Atlas. But titanium was a brittle metal, even though it made the sword lighter to wield than steel, it was susceptible to cracks.

Aiming for the pirate's blade, Joseph struck; chips flying from the edge of it, rendering it less effective. The pirate stepped back, taking in the damage to his blade.

"Oi! That was expensive."

Joseph scoffed. "You were the victim of a swindle then. That blade is worth less than the clothes on your back."

The pirate sneered. "You be talkin' about my good looks, mate?"

Why were pirates always so ill-educated?

Joseph opened his mouth, ready to correct the bilge rat when the pirate's eyes widened, looking over his shoulder. Joseph followed his line of sight to the row of blue coats marching their way.

The Minister's officers had arrived, fending off pirates and helping the civilians put out the fire. The pirates scurried away, seizing what they could from the nearby shops and running back to the shore.

When Joseph returned his gaze, the halfwit was running away. Cowards, the lot of them. Joseph drew his pistol, downing the raider in one shot.

After restoring the smoking pistol to his belt, he rushed to help the officers, until he noticed his own door swinging shut. Some corsair thought they could steal from him?

Joseph huffed, stomping back into his shop, intent on slaying the fool who thought they could pilfer from him.

The first thing he noticed was the absence of the swords on the rack. Weeks of work, stolen within minutes. He breathed out a long breath, until he looked to the mounting on the wall. His father's sword—

Gone.

Of course. Who wouldn't want the finest blade Samsara had to offer?

But the thief was nowhere to be seen.

"Where are you, you thieving rat?"

He stepped a few paces further, checking behind his forging fire and table. It was simple inside his blacksmithing hut, the main room housed his display of new blades and tools for his work, though some of them were thrown to the floor in the thief's urgency. He let out a dissatisfied grunt.

Creaking wood drew his attention back to the door. He caught a glimpse of leather and white cotton before the perpetrator escaped.

He jolted, running to the door and prying it open.

A figure ran into the night, clutching the blade that glinted under the silver light of Davina's moon. Joseph gritted his teeth as he bounded toward the fleeing pirates. One in particular waited for the little thief, but there was something strange about him. Darkness seemed to cling to him like a dark cloud.

Joseph stared after them, even after they made it to the rowboats and to the safety of the lilac sails of *Macha's Demise* beyond. It was Captain Pike and his crew who had raided them tonight. The most fearsome pirate in the Sumerian Sea, though at this point, they were one of the last.

The end of the world had seen to that.

Bodies were strewn across the street, the firelight reflecting dully in their vacant eyes. Only the pirate Joseph had shot down had joined the ranks of the dead along with them.

This is what *they* did. They came to kill, steal, and destroy. Joseph was finished with it. And now, they had taken his father's sword, too. It would be one thing if the Minister had taken it, to either display or destroy.

But a pirate? *Contemptible.*

Joseph looked on at the officers, a group of them gathering to help the surviving citizens. Some assembled to put out the fire, others carried off the injured.

He looked down at his callused soot-stained hands, old burnt skin telling of how much time he spent at the forge. His hands curled into fists. Every second he spent as a blacksmith was agony, reminding him of the family he lost. The joy in the craft had left him years ago.

It was time to leave his father's forge behind. If there was a way to find the pirates, to kill them, and get his sword back, it would be with the Minister's Navy.

And he would find the thief stupid enough to steal from him.

"I've always wanted to sail the seas, been a mighty fine fancy of mine."

Joseph was next in line at the recruitment table. They had lost several officers in the raid and were looking to replenish their ranks, luckily for him.

The Commodore was a poor looking fellow, proving that no amount of finery could mask an unfortunate face. His permanent scowl wasn't helping matters.

Joseph wasn't a tall man, barely making their height requirements, but his arms were bulging. A benefit of smithing and the heavy lifting required of the occupation.

"You're well into your age, old man."

The man in line ahead of him had long white hair that straggled down his back. Joseph assumed the man had run out of working years, money, and food, seeking the Navy for its room and board. Or at least, to die at sea.

"We'd have to toss you overboard for so much as catching a cold. Next." The Commodore rolled his eyes, crossing a line on the parchment before him. He was a tall, proud man, with salt and peppered hair tied back at his nape and bags beneath his gray eyes. Every Samsaran knew Commodore Johnson was not to be trifled with, having nearly three decades sailing the seas, commanding the Navy, and serving the Minister.

Joseph stepped up to the table, glaring down at the Commodore. He knew the man's methods, and while they left much to be desired and respected, he knew the Navy was his best chance at reaching the pirates.

The Commodore sized him up, inspecting him from toe to brow.

"You don't look like much."

"I'm strong and work well with my hands. Not to mention I already know my way around a blade." Joseph delivered his credentials callously. He knew the Commodore could not afford to deny an able-bodied man.

"We'll see about that." Johnson scribbled on the parchment before him. "Tell me, why does the son of a blacksmith want to join the Navy?"

Joseph's fist balled beside him. He *was* a blacksmith, not *only* the son of one. But he knew he'd yet to make a name for himself that wasn't his father's. When he went down in history for killing pirates, that would make Johnson remember him.

"The other night a pirate stole my father's sword. I want it back and I want to kill any pirate that gets in my way."

A cruel smile curved on the side of the Commodore's face.
"Welcome to the Navy, Officer Earhart."

CHAPTER 2
UNDER LILAC SAILS

Angelica stared at her expensive, stolen mirror; one hand pushing her cheek in as she leaned on it. The ship around her was beginning to feel more and more like a prison. Yes, it was her father's ship, but Pike wasn't exactly known to keep decent company.

She really looked nothing like her father, everything must have come from her mother, all of her dark hair, deep warm skin tone and rich brown eyes. Even her full lips and sloped nose were not traits carried by her father. He had a stout nose and thin lips he hid behind a bush of brown and grey. If she had not grown up with the man, she never would have thought them to be related.

It had been too many years since she'd lost her mother. The woman's face had been lost from her memory years ago.

Letting out a sigh, she tied back her curls and stood from her vanity, getting to work on the ties of her corset. The deep red design made her feel like a woman even though she was surrounded by the dirtiest of men. She'd learned to tie her own corsets long ago, not willing to let a crew member touch her long enough to help. She tucked a pistol into the belt at the curve of her waist, covered by her coat.

Finishing up the final touches of her knee-high boots and hat, she walked out to the ship's deck, her newest prize sitting on her hip. She had gone into the blacksmith shop in Samsara hoping for a better sword than the brittle ones her father always gave her. She'd taken one look at the sword on the wall and had to have it. It really was a thing of beauty, a broad blade with a slight curve and the perfect balance on the hilt. It was a shame for it to simply be stored and forgotten on someone's wall.

A sword like that was meant to see battle.

Angelica stepped out onto the deck, blinking at the harsh sunlight and wincing at the smell. The bastards aboard *Macha's Demise* rarely bathed. Her father was not on deck, but that was normal, as he preferred to sit in his study with his grimoire. It was, after all, the very reason he was the most feared pirate on the sea.

Behind the helm stood Guyus, the first mate and her least favorite person. It was clear the entire crew believed she belonged to him. They used to leer at her, making comments about her body the moment she grew curves, but once Guyus had set his shark eyes on her, they had ceased their commentary. She didn't think that was a coincidence.

At least, he was decent enough to wait until she was eighteen to make advances of his own.

It would never happen. Guyus could drown for all she cared.

She avoided his stare, opting to look out to the approaching island, instead. Kheli was a frequent stop for them. It was the one place they didn't raid, instead deciding to rest on the jungle shores. The occupants simply didn't have enough for Pike to raid them. She suspected he held some fondness for the quaint village.

Movement drew her eye to the left. Palden, the youngest crew member and the ship's lookout, joined her on the railing. He was awfully young to be on amongst these miscreants but, like her, he'd hardly had a choice. He was the former first mate's son, and Pike had kept him out of respect for his lost friend.

The boy was some mix between a Moskan and Brettanian,

retaining the dark glow of his father's skin in the harsh sun that wearied seafarers. He came up to Angelica's shoulder, tall for his age, but it was his round face that gave away his youth.

There was an apple rounding his vest pocket. He was not the most skilled thief.

"Getting into trouble, I see?"

Palden's face reddened, putting one hand over his pocket. "I missed breakfast, alright? Captain's got me sleeping in the crow's nest. It's so cold and high up. I hardly slept a wink."

Angelica fought a smile. It was for the best he slept there; it kept the rest of the crew from messing with him.

"Didn't sleep, yet you missed breakfast?"

He blinked at her. "Well, I stole the basket, shouldn't I get an extra apple every so often? Ya know, as a tax?"

She turned around, facing the boy whose face was scrunched in anger. She hoped he wasn't so bold as to complain to the rest of the crew, but she enjoyed his honesty. It was refreshing. Though she did catch a sneer from Old Rob, the ship's rigger. His distaste could only go so far, given his replaceable position, but a poor choice could leave Palden with a few bruises.

"Don't think the rest of the crew will see it that way."

He frowned deeply, following Angelica's gaze to the rigger. Luckily, he had his hands full, preparing the ship to weigh anchor.

She put a hand on Palden's shoulder. "When you're strong enough to hold yourself in a fight you can claim as many apples as you want."

His face lit up at the notion, then he pushed his sleeve up to show Angelica his arm. "Look, I'm getting strong already." Indeed, the stick of his arm looked a bit fuller than it had previously.

"Good." She reached out, fluffing his curly hair. "You'll need it." His smile sunk when his eyes caught on to something behind her.

"There you are, *cariño*." Guyus slipped up beside her on the rail, too close for a casual conversation. She cursed herself for not seeing him coming, or at least expecting it. He came to torment her every chance he got, and he was most bold when her father was not on deck. "I hope you aren't getting any headstrong ideas."

Palden took off before Guyus could punish him for lingering too long.

"I could tell you the same," she sneered, shrugging off the hand he had placed on her shoulder. She'd made it clear she wasn't interested, but that seemed to encourage him.

A mischievous smile painted his face. He was tall, towering a foot over her; a fact he used to his advantage. He leaned over her to box her against the railing, pushing her against it until his front was firmly pressed to her backside.

She growled at him. The fact that he would be so brazen in front of the entire crew was humiliating. Angelica had spent years acquiring some semblance of respect from the crew and Guyus was managing to erase all of that with every interaction they had. She should know better than to let him corner her.

"Come now, we both know this is only a matter of time." His fingertips slipped down her arm, resting on her hand while his other hand lifted a lock of her hair to smell it. He was oddly fascinated by her scent. Angelica bit her tongue to keep it from telling him *exactly* how revolting that was. "I even waited until you were a marriageable age." Like he deserved some prize for it.

She snapped an elbow back, hitting his ribs and causing him to jolt back. He grunted, holding his side when Angelica faced him.

"I am not your prize, Guyus."

"Angelica." The sharp tone of her father's voice made her jolt, his tone telling her all she needed to know. His face confirmed as much, with the way his lips pressed together and his brow furrowed. "Come here."

Angelica lifted her head, refusing to cower under his overwhelming attention.

She followed her father into his study, a smile tipping her lips as she witnessed Guyus attempt to straighten. The study resided in the space below the quarterdeck, across from his bedchamber.

Pike kept his back to her as he spoke, lighting a candle. His signature smoldering coat laid across the back of his chair.

His hair was long and frizzed around his head, with occasional braids and beaded jewels strung through it. His beard was closely kept to his face, seeming to be the lone part of his hygiene he cared about, contrasting against the rest of his rough features.

Tattoos peaked out from beneath his shirt, on his forearms and neck. Angelica didn't understand why he didn't show the tattoos more. They were arguably more terrifying than the smoldering coat. Every time he cast one of Her bloody spells or curses, a tattoo would appear on his flesh.

The design of rippling smoke around his neck was for the spell he cast on his coat, but that one was to intimidate his enemies and remind his crew what he was capable of. The rest were a branding of his darkest deeds.

She glared at a spot on his hand, almost indistinguishable from other age spots there, but the small star was there because of her. Of the night she had tried to run–

"Do you know why you are here, Angelica?"

She snapped out of her racing thoughts, focusing on the question. She didn't have a specific role because she helped with whatever was needed. She could tend to the ship, hoist sails, patch up wounds, clean and maintain weaponry, count treasure— "Because I'm your daughter and a pirate."

He breathed in heavily. "Because you are my daughter. That's precisely it. I allow you to remain here because you are my daughter."

That's not what she had meant, but it would be foolish to correct him.

He turned to her. "The world is dying, my child. No one will take you in. Not Samsara. Not those poor villagers on Kheli. Do you think any of them want a pirate's daughter wandering around them? No, they have mouths to feed, and you'll be the first to suffer when food is scarce."

Angelica knew the world was suffering and their raids made it worse. Unfortunately, that made her the enemy to everyone save Pike. Still, she could find a way to blend in if the situation called for it.

His hand landed on a large leather bound book with scribbled notes surrounding it; the grimoire. The very thing keeping her on that ship.

"I care for you. I feed you. I make sure no one hurts you and this is how you repay me?" Angelica stayed silent, her hands squeezing together in her lap. "Even still, you've yet to provide me with a grandson–"

Angelica had to snap her eyes closed to keep them from glaring at him. His precious grand-*son*. Like she needed more reasons to hate their gender entirely. Even the dalliances she had taken part in had been strategically timed to prevent such results, since he wouldn't allow her to take the witch's tonic.

"I may not always be there to protect you. Guyus can ensure your survival when I cannot." He straightened himself, gathering patience she also had to find. "I chose him as my first mate, which means you need to respect him. You may not choose to accept him, but he is *my* choice." His voice raised, and she flinched. "I will not be disrespected by my own daughter!"

She closed her eyes, expecting the back of his hand that didn't come. Not today, it would seem. As long as she could keep her tongue under control.

"Maybe you should choose a better first mate," she mumbled.

The slap came before she could register it, flinging her head to the side.

"My choices will not be questioned. Is that understood?"

She swallowed her pride and a little of her dignity. "Yes, father."

Pike breathed out, his voice softening. "You know I don't like hurting you, Angelica. Don't make me do it again."

"Yes, father." She stared at the floor, not trusting herself enough to look him in the eye.

He grunted, a reaction she had come to know as satisfaction, then he fell to his chair, deflating as if the world was on his shoulders. "One more thing. I've chosen to take Kheli as a port. You remember the state of the last one."

Angelica nodded. Their last port was set on one of the small islands leading to Kalon. Necromites had floated on the water's surface, surviving in their inhuman forms long enough to overrun it. Five crew members were lost in the melee.

But Kheli?

"Forgive me, Captain. But isn't Kheli controlled by Samsara?"

Though they raided Samsara often, it was too populated, too manned to be a good place to stay long. Not to mention the witch community that didn't take kindly to Pike's presence. After all, he was the example of why a witch's son wasn't allowed to reach maturity.

"Precisely." He pointed at Angelica, excitement brightening his kohl lined eyes. "Samsara depends on the little island for its food. If we control its greatest resource, we control Samsara." A glint appeared in the corner of his eye. She knew that look; a bit of his power hungry madness coming to the surface. He'd always wanted Samsara.

"And the Navy?" He waved her off like her concern wasn't valid, but the Navy was the entire reason they never took Kheli before.

"We've been thinning them out for years. They can only send so many people to Kheli at once."

Angelica's jaw opened to argue further, but his hand came up before them, halting her. "My mind is made." She nodded, knowing any further argument would result in swift punishment.

But taking Kheli? It was madness. Either they would be crushed by the Navy or they would cause the deaths of countless civilians on Samsara.

The thought made her sick. It was bad enough that it happened so often during raids.

She turned to leave, but he left her with a parting phrase.

"I will see you and Guyus married, Angelica." Not a question. No room for argument.

"Yes, father."

Too bad she wouldn't remain with them long enough to fulfill that promise.

CHAPTER 3

THE RULE OF THREES

The sky was cloudless as the ship approached Kheli. The mighty Davina's Will had glittering silver sails and a near luminescent hull. It created a shimmering halo in the water around the ship as the sun bounced off it.

Joseph had never ventured off Samsara before. The dreary rains of the island left much to be desired, but with the sun on his face and the wind in his hair, he could get used to this. Whether it was sailing or the beautiful spot of green creeping in from the horizon.

Kheli.

It was a trading destination for Samsara. The only one, really. With most of the world dead, walled up, or on strict border policies, there was little goods to be obtained. But Samsara wasn't viable for reaping crops. The ground was too rocky and wet to grow much besides spots of trees and grass.

They relied on Kheli for most of their fruits and vegetables.

Sounds of a Navy ship preparing to dock chorused around him.

"Get ready to weigh anchor!" The Commodore shouted from his perch on the quarter deck before the helm. The ship's wheel spun behind him. The image of a fiery bird with outstretched wings decorated the helm's center. From Davinian mythology, the phoenix could eviscerate hoards of necromites with a single strike.

Though the phoenix was nothing more than a story, the villainous creatures were very much real. The bite of a necromite would sentence one to death, possessing the body and spreading its disease.

Those creatures existed on the mainland, unseen by Samsarans. The threat on Kheli was pirates, fearsome men who didn't take pity on the innocent. That was the purpose of the Navy, to protect the people of both islands from raids.

Joseph learned the three-rule code that the Minister's Navy lived by on his first day. One: to abandon your crew was to enlist with Hell. Two: your appearance is your control. Do not lose it. Three: protect the people by whatever means necessary.

The code was punishable in varying degrees, but every officer knew deserters were not to be tolerated.

That had been a couple weeks ago. There hadn't been very extensive training, but it seemed the Navy was low on recruits. Captain Pike and his crew raided the Navy ships often, killing anyone who was in their way.

Joseph rushed to the mast, handling the rigging and rolling back the sails to slow their approach to the dock. It made the entrance easier for when the anchor was dropped. In the midst of his duties, it was hard not to stare at the beautiful lush green jungle that made up Kheli, contrasting with the light blue sky and dark waters.

He'd never seen so much green in his life.

"First time, sailor?"

Joseph's gaze snapped to the man who spoke. A sea weathered man who seemed more inclined to salty water and sails than dry land. His piercing gaze was light blue, blinking through white lashes. The nautical cap he wore was several seasons too old and disheveled. Joseph could count half a dozen infractions on his appearance alone, but the man didn't seem to care.

"Yes, is it that obvious?"

The man smirked, revealing a set of yellowed teeth. "Ya 'ave a wonderin' look 'bout ya. Like that island 'as every secret the world could 'ave."

There weren't many places Joseph thought he would see and all of them were on Samsara. Just to see an island that was not his own was a rare gem itself.

"Any story book fantasy ya be havin' 'bout that island, drown them in the sea now." The man pulled a small flask from his coat pocket. Another infraction. He downed the liquid then sniffed. "The people there be savages. I'm tellin' ya." He sniffed again, staring at the approaching land. "Stay close to the officers," he paused, reaching a hand out to grasp the air before Joseph's face. "Or they'll snatch ya."

Joseph flinched and the man bellowed. Unfortunately for him, that drew attention to the flask he still grasped.

"This is your last warning, Hopkins." A young freckled man with honey brown hair tied back at his nape and a pristine uniform snatched the flask from the drunkard. "If I catch you with anything like this again, you'll be discharged for good. No ship captain would even touch you."

"Yes, Lieutenant," he responded half-heartedly, returning to his duty at the mast. It was a lenient punishment, but Ashby was known to be merciful and just.

It made him well liked among the officers.

Lieutenant Sebastian Ashby.

The rumors claimed he was in line for the position of Commodore.

Him and—

"Lieutenant Ashby!" The Commodore called, even more heated than he normally was. Which was saying something since he possessed a permanent scowl.

The lieutenant straightened, stepping up to his Commodore and saluting. "Yes, sir."

The Commodore gritted his teeth like Ashby's perfect form

offended him. "Get your little *pet* in line or it will be *your* head to pay."

"Right away, sir." Ashby saluted again, dismissing himself to do the task assigned. At the back edge of the ship, a crowd gathered, staring behind the ship rather than gaping at the new island. Apparently, there was something far more interesting.

Joseph leaned against the rail of the ship, looking to the ship's wake right when a great shout echoed across the waves.

Behind the ship, being dragged along by a rope attached to a plank of wood and a sail, was the other candidate for Commodore.

Lieutenant James Hawkins.

He shouted again in a joy so pure, it resonated with the entire crew. They cheered him on from the rails of the ship. The plank of wood he surfed crested a wave, gaining air before drafting down again. The sail he'd attached to it made the contraption fly.

Ashby leaned on the quarterdeck rail, glaring down at his friend and shouting, "Get your ass on the ship, Hawkins."

"Make me!" He shouted over the rush of waves.

Ashby huffed, freeing a knife from his coat pocket. "I will cut the line and we won't come back for you. You'll be swimming to Kheli."

A cackling kind of laugh escaped the wind bound lieutenant before he shifted a few things on his sail and wood contraption. Then, propelled by a large wave, he launched into the air with a great shout. The men cheered as he gained more air than any of them had thought possible.

Crack.

The wood plank below him fell to the waves, slapping the sea water. But the loss of weight helped Hawkins gain more air. The rope was wrapped around his waist while he gripped a staff that secured the edges of the sail. He used the staff in tandem with the wind, gliding him closer to the ship deck.

The moment his feet hit the deck, he tumbled across it, rolling in a splatter, but laughing loudly.

"Did you see that, Bash? It worked!"

"Yes, yes. We all saw. Are you trying to get us kicked off this mission?" He reached for his friend. They clasped forearms as James was raised from the deck. His uniform was in complete contrast to Ashby's. His coat was missing entirely, his shirt was unbuttoned, revealing a hairy chest beneath, and of course, he was soaking wet. Somehow, he managed to keep his cap on. "You're a mess," Ashby chastised.

James turned up his nose at Ashby mockingly. "And you're too clean."

There was a split second of tension between the two before they broke out into laughter.

The Commodore sneered in disgust. "The pair of you are pathetic." The laughter ceased, most of the crew returning to their docking stations before they could be told to do so. "If I could, I would discharge you so disgracefully even the butcher houses wouldn't take you."

James' lips curved into a knowing smile. "But you can't." The Commodore sneered harder, flicking his eyes up and down. "Only the Minister has the ability to rid the Navy of us and he won't because he wants one of us to take *your* job."

Joseph swore the lieutenant had a death wish.

"I can still make your lives a living hell in the meantime, Lieutenant. Do not. Test me," he hissed. The Commodore turned his back on the men, a clear dismissal. Much to Joseph's displeasure, their eyes met. "Back to work, sailor."

Joseph grunted, returning to his spot at the mast next to Hopkins. A quick look back and his eyes caught on a pair of dark blue ones.

James Hawkins studied him through heavy dark lashes, a slight smile curving his mouth. People talked about him, quite a bit. They spoke of his bravery, his charisma and wit, but mostly the magnetic pull he had.

"Pirates!"

All heads snapped to the crow's nest where the lookout was pointing out to sea.

"On the portside! It's *Macha's Demise*!"

Heads leaned off the portside to get a glimpse, but they needn't have gone so far. The ship barreled by, a force rocking into *Davina's Will* and tossing the officers off balance.

"They've attached themselves to us!"

Joseph leaned off the rail to see metal spikes hammering into the side of the ship. Weeks of damage being inflicted in a manner of seconds. One storm would sink them.

He looked up in time to jump away as a grappling hook seized the rail he was on. Pirates swung from masts, climbing on from their hooks, others were setting up a gangplank to walk across. The siege was in full force. How had the pirates arrived so quickly without anyone noticing?

Joseph pulled a military grade saber from its sheath, facing a particularly nasty pirate as he flopped onto the deck with a dirty grin. As far as pirates went, this man was entirely average. A short glance at the pirate's frail sword told him this was not his little thief. They crossed blades for a moment before Joseph pushed him off the edge to the sea between the ships, the man's shrill scream echoing along the hull.

But the short victory could not be celebrated when pirates surrounded them. It was becoming clear that they were vastly outnumbered.

"You must be new," one pirate drawled, a higher hitch to his voice than most. "I 'aven't seen you around yet."

Joseph gave him a mockingly short bow. "If you survive, you'll have to get used to my face."

"Oi, it's not your face that's the problem. You're a bit shorter than most officers." The pirate turned his head quizzically. Joseph had come to terms with his height years ago. He found it made men underestimate him and he wouldn't be giving up that advantage.

Joseph turned his head, assessing the pirate. "You've got something here." He pointed to his own chin.

"Do I?" The pirate lowered his sword, using his free hand to wipe at his chin.

Joseph struck, aiming to take back the naval sword in the pirate's hand. The pirate drew back, but not far enough. A few more strikes and the pirate fell backwards, landing on his ass, the sword sliding away from his hand.

He reached for it, but Joseph was quicker, his boot landing on the broad side of the saber.

"I'd suggest leaving my sword alone."

The pirate narrowed his eyes, but bolted away when he came to terms with being unarmed. Joseph sighed at the man's cowardice. This was Pike's fearless crew?

As the thought formed, a clashing of metal met at his ear, too bloody close.

Ashby was there, deflecting a pirate's advance and fending him away from Joseph.

"Back to work, officer."

Joseph lunged, picking up the pirate's lost sword. He'd practiced with two swords before. It required more strength than a man usually possessed. Luckily, Joseph was built like an ox.

He took up Ashby's back, crossing two blades at once. A feat he wasn't confident in, but he hardly had a choice now. The pirates sensed his lack of efficiency, inching in on him. Joseph strained with the weight of two men bearing down on him.

Hawkins came up behind one of the men, tapping the pirate on the shoulder.

The man turned and Hawkins was smiling, a belt buckle in his hand. "I do think you misplaced this."

The pirate scrambled as his pants fell down his legs and he tripped in his rush to fix them. Hawkins landed one boot on the man's ass before pushing him over the nearby railing. The man screamed all the way down.

Joseph and the other pirate had stopped fighting to watch, forgetting themselves for a moment before the pirate struck. Joseph caught it in time, but the pirate was outnumbered now. Ashby had defeated his own foe, taking up their side. The pirate, clearly seeing how he was unmatched, jumped off the railing himself.

"Not bad, sailor," Hawkins said, slapping a hand on Joseph's back.

"Any man left in the water better learn to swim." Pike's booming voice was unmistakable, his disappointment and anger in his own crew for failing clear. "If I see any of you again, I will cut your miserable throats."

Joseph leaned over the railing to see Pike on his own ship. He hadn't even bothered to cross. At his side, a gangly fellow with a dark scraggly beard, and his other side, the most beautiful woman he had ever seen.

Just by her rigid posture, Joseph could tell she was a force to be reckoned with, strong, fierce, wild, and untamable. He'd never been more attracted to someone in his life. Her ebony hair glistened in the sunlight, her dark sepia skin contrasting with the white of her shirt and the red of her corset. He wished she would look at him, just once, but he wasn't so much as graced with a glance.

But as his eyes traveled down her frame, they caught on the sword on her hip, and the gold crusted into the hilt. He'd stared at that sword for years; he'd recognize it anywhere.

Joseph's jaw hardened, his teeth grinding.

She was his little thief.

CHAPTER 4

GHOST STORIES

The officers set up camp off shore beside the village.

Some of the villagers had been hospitable. A blonde woman and her large burly husband were the first to greet everyone, their accents similar to Hopkins'. It made Joseph wonder what could possibly have caused the drunkard's opinion of them. In truth, Joseph felt as if he'd been played for a fool.

It wasn't until he felt their disdainful glares that he understood. These people did not like officers, that much was clear, but not the reason why.

He put the glares behind him as he set up his tent and retrieved food from a very grumpy cook. It was truly a feat, the number of muscles alone it took for a man to frown *that* deeply. His messy apron was splattered with juices from the grits he'd made and dished out, communicating in grunts and huffs.

Joseph took his dinner without complaint.

The chief and his wife had offered the officers fresh fruit upon their arrival, filling his belly enough that he wasn't hungry for anything more. But he knew better than to offend the cook by skipping.

He plopped down on a log next to a billowing fire, accompanying four other officers including Hopkins, who leaned his back against the log picking at his teeth.

Joseph scanned the crowd, searching for the two lieutenants who had fought with him. Instinct told him those were the men to be with if he wanted a chance at getting his father's sword back. They seemed to be in the center of the action, which was precisely where Joseph needed to be.

Hawkins and Ashby were, however, nowhere to be seen. He sat down while the officers were mid-conversation.

"No, I'm telling you. I saw something in the water last night. I looked over the side and a sea creature bigger than the ship swam under us." The man was scrawny with a patch on his coat for over five years in service. The Navy usually packed its officers with muscles as soon as possible, but the training seemed to have missed this one.

"Eh, you're jumping at bloody shadows," Daryl replied, shoveling grits into his mouth like it was his last meal. Joseph had been given the pleasure of bunking with the crude man on the voyage to Kheli. He spoke in his sleep, mostly profanities.

"Am not," the scrawny man huffed. "I saw it with my own eyes! It had arms bigger than the masts trailing behind it and several of them. Not just one or two."

"No, he's right," Hopkins spoke up, drawing the two men's attention. "I've seen it. A massive creature with glowin' eyes on the side of its bulbous head. Its arms are tentacles with cups that suck the skin from your bones and layers of teeth so sharp it can bite a hole straight into the bottom of a ship."

Both men gulped.

"What is it?"

"Nemain's personal attack dog," Hopkins whispered. A shiver coursed through the scrawny one. "The locals call him Hufgufa. They say he wraps his tentacles around a ship, splittin' it in 'alf and feastin' on the sailors who fall in its jaws. Mark my words, one day it'll be comin' to drag us down to the depths of the sea."

Silence encircled the camp, leaving the cracking of the fire.

Hopkins burst out laughing at their dumbstruck faces. "It's just a story, lads." He leaned over to wink at Joseph.

The other men breathed out as if they wouldn't have taken another breath if it had been true, but Joseph wasn't in the business of believing ghost stories.

He finished off his grits and stood to return his bowl to the cook. The man would rage if every single one wasn't properly returned.

He let the bowl clank against the other dirty ones behind the cook's pot, sending a bemused smile to the man who grunted happily at the obedience.

Joseph felt a prickle of awareness that someone was watching him. He turned his head to see James Hawkins leaning against a tree and smirking. His uniform was put right before they had docked in Kheli. No doubt, he'd had help from Ashby, but the devilish glint to his eyes couldn't be helped.

He turned, disappearing behind the tree and into the jungle. The sun was down and Macha's lilac moon shone over the ground making the juggle beyond impossibly dark.

Joseph's feet started moving before he could coherently make the decision to follow as if there was a string tugging him forward.

It wasn't clear where he was going, but every few steps, he caught a glimpse of a phantom in the trees guiding him where he needed to go.

Village lights came into view, revealing small huts and a grassy courtyard in the center. In the middle of it was the Maiden herself, a stone statue of Macha.

Hawkins' silhouette disappeared behind a nearby hut, but a glint of lilac in his peripherals drew Joseph's attention to the sea. Was the light playing tricks on his mind, or was there something out there?

"Enjoying the scenery?"

Joseph's attention dragged to Hawkins, his brows scrunching together. "Yeah, something like that."

A larger figure strode up behind him, the sheer build of him taking over Hawkins' leaner frame. Ashby surveyed Joseph with the critical eye he was all too familiar with. It was usually followed by an infraction of some sort. He tugged at his coat by instinct.

"Are you sure about this?" Ashby's tone was clipped, brittle.

Hawkins eyed Joseph too, but it wasn't critical or negative. James looked at him like he was searching for something. Then a grin split his lips.

"I'm sure. He's one of us." Joseph blinked, unsure what he meant by that. James tipped his head to the building behind them. "Follow us."

The building Joseph followed James into could hardly be called that. Planks of wood, mostly driftwood, made up the walls and a thick layer of large dried tree leaves covered the top. The structure didn't make sense, yet it worked.

Inside, village people were packed in, talking to one another in hushed tones. They failed to notice as three naval officers snuck in and took up positions on the back wall. It seemed odd to be joining in whatever was happening. There was a strange urgency building in the atmosphere, as if their volcano was about to erupt.

Davina, he hoped not.

The large man who had greeted the Navy at the dock stood at a makeshift dais on the other end of the building. The moment he stepped up, the room quieted, eager to hear what their chief had to say. He was a middle-aged man, with clear brown eyes and a sad smile curving his lips.

"My friends," he started and the people held their breath. "The Commodore be tellin' me today—" He paused, taking a breath to steady himself. "Bah, I'll just be gettin' done with it then. Any man 'tween the ages of sixteen and thirty-five be required to join the Minister's Navy."

The room sat in shocked silence, until it detonated. Screams and shouts pelted the air, filling it so much, it was difficult to make out the words they said. The general consensus was outrage, and Joseph couldn't blame them. They were their own island, in need of their own people to help protect them.

The chief raised his arms, motioning them to quiet.

"I know ya be angry, but be givin' no other choice." The man sounded defeated as if he already visited any other possible roads and came back empty handed.

"Make them leave!" One man shouted, standing from his seat. "We owe them nothing. What has the Minister done for us?"

Joseph felt larger than he was in that room with people who had good reason to hate him.

"All they do is take!"

A man pointed back to where the three of them stood, their backs to the plank wall. Hawkins leaned against it with a bored expression, but up close there was tension in his jaw.

"Run them out and we can provide for ourselves." The people shouted in agreement, firing up their hostility.

"But they cannot!" The chief bellowed. The room grew silent again. They had clear respect for the chief, even if they didn't like the news he delivered. "Don't you see? They be needin' our island and what we provide. Samsara not be light in population. If we do not obey, they won't be needin' us. They'd slaughter every one of us and station Samsarans in our stead."

The room grew deathly quiet. Joseph's heart sank like a rock in the ocean. He'd never thought the Minister could be so cruel. Genocide was a large step to take, but Samsara would perish without the food Kheli provided. When had peaceful trade been taken off the table? Maybe it had to do with the pirates attacking their ships.

"Lads, ladies," he continued, defeated. "We have no choice."

The room devolved into whispers. It was their families on the line. Even with their leader's explanation, more than a few heads turned to glare at the three officers.

The chief let himself down from the dais, making his way to the back of the building where they stood, Hawkins launching off the wall to meet the chief first.

"A word," the chief said before shuffling away from them to the door. They quickly followed. Eyes trailed them from the room. Anger, hate, and suspicion weighed heavily on him, making his skin crawl.

Once outside, the chief pulled them into the tree line.

"We have visitors," the chief blew out and Hawkins froze.

"For how long?" Ashby bit out. The chief eyed Joseph.

"You can trust him, Roger."

Judging by Ashby's wrinkled brow, he didn't agree, but Roger seemed to trust Hawkins enough for the both of them.

"They arrived a fortnight ago. They be takin' from the farms on the Northside."

Hawkins shook his head, his black hair tumbling with him. "Did you tell the Commodore?"

Roger huffed out a laugh. "Like he be inclined to help us." Roger's face fell. "Aye, and all he be tellin' me was that it be my job to be takin' care of them." He brought a rolled joint to his mouth and lit it with a match he had in his pocket. "This be me, takin' care of it." He motioned with his free hand to officers before him.

Ashby bit his lip. "Have you tried to negotiate? Maybe we could set up borders."

"And share the island?" Roger laughed, but it was hollow. "Better men have tried, my boy."

Ashby's face turned to stone. Many emotions twirled in Joseph's stomach, disappointment in the Navy for neglecting a people they use, anger at their inclination to take what protection the villagers had, and hope—

Joseph recalled the lilac glint he saw on the sea earlier. One that wasn't a reflection of the moon. *Pirates.* He'd bet his life on it that Pike and his crew had anchored off shore. If they were here, so was his father's sword.

"Our men be loadin' onto that ship by mornin'," Roger explained. "Find a way to stay behind. Smuggle yourselves if you must. We be needin' you here."

Hawkins nodded. "You have my word."

Roger turned his eyes to Ashby who nodded in turn. "Mine as well."

Then, the chief's eyes landed on Joseph, testing him. He didn't see a reason to hesitate.

"Mine too."

The chief let out a satisfied grunt. "I be countin' on the lot of ya." Roger shuffled back to the growing shouts in the building behind them.

Hawkins whipped around, a smile on his face. "I told you."

"Proves nothing," Ashby retorted.

"What?" Joseph asked, suddenly lost. The entire experience had him forgetting that he was a trained officer and these were his superiors. "Sir," he added quickly.

Hawkins threw an arm over his shoulder. "We're past that now. Earhart, was it?"

"Joseph, sir."

Ashby crossed his arms in front of himself. "You will still address us as 'sir' when we are around any other members of the Navy, but if you continue to do so while we are alone, James will throw a fit."

"I will not," he protested.

Joseph blinked, shoving the lieutenant's arm off while shaking his head. "Wait, wait." He rubbed his head. "What is this?" He motioned to the three of them.

"Fate," James said immediately.

"Idiocy," Ashby corrected.

"An adventure."

"A suicide mission."

James glared at his friend, who's stoic expression was hard to penetrate. "It depends on how you look at it." Joseph shook his head again. "Look," James said, taking a step forward. "These people need us. If we get on that ship tomorrow, they could be dead by the time we get back."

"These strangers, they'll want the island to themselves." Ashby's tone stayed steady, emotionless.

Joseph was counting on it. He considered the consequences of telling them his real motivations, but a lack of a moral compass seemed like a good way to get his ass shoved on that ship tomorrow.

James took his silence as hesitance.

"Think about it," James continued. "If you get on that ship tomorrow, I won't blame you. You don't know these people and I know we're asking a lot from you, but—"

"I'm with you," Joseph interrupted, perhaps too quickly.

James' smile tipped to the side with the confidence of someone who's used to getting their way, but it was Ashby's eyes that narrowed.

After accepting a handshake from James, Joseph felt the finality of his decision and what it could cost him.

"Off to bed. We'll see you tomorrow."

***

Carts of food; fruits, barley, potatoes were loaded into the ship, overfilling it to the point of combusting. They really should have sailed a second ship, even though *Nemain's Revenge* rarely ventured past the docks of Samsara.

Joseph was awestruck with the sheer number of plants and crops that could grow on Kheli. It seemed impossible, given how lacking Samsara's soil was that Kheli was blessed with such a harvest. The only caveat was the island's land mass. There simply wasn't enough of it to use properly. Although the soil was good, the dangerous terrain, proximity to the volcano, and many other factors prevented them from farming in the heart of the jungle.

Most of the farms were kept on the flatter southern end of the island.

With the growth of population on Samsara, and the fact that the Navy was seizing nearly half of its workers, the farms were needed more than ever.

James slammed his palms on the Commodore's desk, quivering a quill and ink pot.

"This is ridiculous. Those men are needed here."

The Commodore didn't even glance up from the food reports in his hands. The air was brisk today, the tent around them flapping in the wind.

James had dragged Joseph from his tent, explaining very little before they had ended up in the Commodore's tent. Joseph's guess was that he remained for support or testimony, though there wasn't much he could truly say.

"Mr. Hawkins. I suggest you remember your place."

"Those men are Kheli's only protection when the Navy isn't here, not to mention they are farmers, not fighters. They need to work the fields that supply both islands."

The Commodore finally set down his papers. "I offered to send replacement farmers. The *chief* of this island assured me that the women would be able to handle the crops on their own. Is that not true?"

It didn't take a mastermind to determine the chief sought to protect his people, and replacement farmers were enough of a threat to a group of unprotected women. Roger likely thought it was better to overwork the remaining women than see them in danger from strangers. It was both logical and absurd, neither answer preferable. Joseph didn't envy the choices Roger had to make for his people.

James' eyes hardened, giving nothing away, deciding to support Roger's choice.

"And what of their protection? Those pirates we encountered earlier are on the island."

The Commodore's cold eyes widened, but somehow it was too controlled to be surprise.

"Would you leave the island for the pirates to take over? What will you do then if Captain Pike seizes Samsara's main food source?"

"We'll take it back. The Navy outnumbers the pirates fifty to one. We'd take them down in a single night and we'll have replacement farmers to the island the next day."

Joseph's heart sank. "You would sacrifice an entire village? For what? Convenience?"

The Commodore's eyes lowered, narrowing at Joseph. "Who are you to question me, sailor?" His hand raised, pointing a finger at James. "I may put up with this one, but you have no authority here. Get back in line."

"He's here on my authority."

The Commodore glared at James. "Don't push me, Hawkins."

James leaned forward, inches from the Commodore's face. "Don't push me, *Commodore*." They stared at each other a moment longer, until the Commodore straightened, gaining some distance.

"Fine, you care so much about them, you stay. Keep your pet and the other insolent lieutenant. If I find the pirates have taken or destroyed the crops in any way by the time I get back, it'll be your necks in a noose in place of the pirates'. Is that clear?"

James straightened. "Clear as a favorable sky."

He turned and Joseph caught the smile curving his face. This was much easier for them than smuggling themselves off the ship.

"Now we have work to do."

CHAPTER 5

WHAT LUCK IS THIS?

Angelica blinked at the brightness of sunlight reflecting off the sea's calm waters. It was rare to see Her so calm. A ship with glistening silver sails was preparing to set sail, boxes of goods being lifted onto the deck with a small army of village men. They weren't dressed as officers. They weren't even dressed for sailing, yet they were corralled onto *Davina's Will* like a prison march.

"What gift is this?" Guyus murmured from her side, causing her to drop the scope from her eyes to watch him. He stood with his overinflated pride, his chest puffing out, one hand on his hip, the other on his scope, no doubt coming to the same conclusion as Angelica had.

"They're actually foolish enough to take the island's means of defense? Not that it was much, anyway. They must know we're here, yet they leave the island to us."

Angelica felt her irritation grow, with Guyus, Samsara's Minister, or the hand of Davina herself, she didn't know. It was foolish, especially since the men were leaving behind their women, elders, and children. Pike wouldn't hesitate to seize control. And *that* didn't bode well for her plans to escape.

"Why would they just leave like that?"

"Does it matter?" Guyus snapped his scope shut, turning to Angelica with a huge grin. "The island is ours. We'll be claiming huts by the end of the day." Guyus reached out a hand, aiming for her cheek. "You can share mine, sweetheart."

She slapped the hand away before it could even brush her skin. "It's too easy."

Angelica thought about what her father said about not resisting the first mate, but there weren't any other crewmates around to witness his rejection. By the smirk twisting his face, he enjoyed her sharpness. Her breakfast spoiled in her gut at the thought that it had pleased him.

"Kheli is a main food source for Samsara. There is no way they would leave it unprotected without good reason. We best keep our eyes and ears open."

Guyus' smirk deepened, as if he hadn't heard a word she said. Fine, he could die by the Navy's hand. It wouldn't bother her in the slightest.

Angelica returned her eye to her scope, sensing his hand in time to smack it off her waist. An unpleasant shiver ran up her spine.

Movement at the docks drew her attention, a small, lithe figure ran down the dock, running into the arms of one of the village men. He caught the small child cradling the figure tightly. A woman ran after the child, but instead of pulling the child away from him, she fell into the man's arms next, the three of them embracing like it was the last time they would. It very well could be.

Angelica couldn't decide which one of them was more in danger.

Something about the men being transported to Samsara was unsettling to her. Whatever this was, it was important enough for the Minister to separate families.

"Something about this isn't right."

"It's a horrible decision on their part, but an impassable opportunity for us."

Angelica lowered her scope as naval officers forcibly pulled the family apart. It made her see outstretched arms as they were pulled from her own and an arm around her small forearm, dragging her away. A long buried hurt rose to the surface so fast she had to clear her throat to avoid a sob.

"We need to report back to the Captain."

CHAPTER 6
MONKEY BUSINESS

Watching the ship leave the dock left a pit at the bottom of Joseph's stomach. Something about the men leaving seemed entirely *wrong*. Warning bells rang in his head during the interaction, but he dismissed it as the Minister's stupidity for leaving the island unprotected.

His gaze traveled to Ashby and he remembered that it wasn't entirely true. The island was being defended by three unprepared officers.

A few weeks ago Joseph had no naval training, had never been off Samsara, and now he was risking his life for a *damn* sword.

He was beginning to agree with Ashby's sentiments, maybe this was a suicide mission.

"Roger is getting the remaining villagers together," Ashby said with a sigh. The men were loaded onto that ship an hour ago. Many of the women and children left behind were still grieving the sudden absence of their loved ones. That concerned wrinkle between Ashby's eyebrows was not because of their grief. "I pray they can assemble some means of protecting themselves in the case of our failure."

"We won't fail."

Ashby let out a gruff laugh. "Confidence won't earn us more men."

Joseph crossed his arms, forcing his face into neutral boredom. "Sir, I believe it to be Pike's crew we are facing."

The lieutenant's head whipped to him so quickly, his hair slapped against his shoulder. "How did you come to that conclusion?"

"I saw the ship. It could have been the light of the moon, but I could've sworn I saw lilac sails." The irony didn't escape Joseph that the most feared pirate in these waters was affiliated with a color so soft and delicate that it was associated with flowers and moonlight.

Ashby's jaw ticked as the wheels of his head turned. "Once James gets back, we'll take a walk to the Northside, see what we're dealing with."

"Where did he go?" James had disappeared hours ago.

Ashby shrugged. "When your brother says 'I'll be right back' then shoots into the jungle like his life depends on it, you learn to hold your questions."

A rustle of leaves captured Joseph's attention. The thick jungle did let enough light through to identify the lone figure walking their way. His hand landed on the pommel of his sword.

Ashby put a hand before him.

It wasn't long before a smirk was visible on the familiar face. "I'm afraid I'll only provide you with more questions, brother." James appeared no different, his officer uniform intact, even if he did unbutton the top portion in the sweltering island heat.

"And where exactly did you run off to?" Ashby's hand relaxed and so did Joseph's, dangling at his side.

James' answer– a single raised eyebrow and a turned head. "You can come out now, Robin."

A small chirping noise came from the closest tree, before a small brown hairball with a tail emerged from behind it, his curious eyes wide.

A monkey?

His eyes scanned each one of them, a healthy dose of apprehension filling his gaze when he laid eyes on Joseph. There was something intelligent about his eyes that Joseph had never seen in an animal before.

Robin serged towards James, running up his arm until he landed on his shoulder. It was a beautiful hairy beast with a white face, a brownish gray body, and a long tail that wrapped around James' arm for stability.

"No wandering off next time, Robin." The creature's mouth formed an "O" shape as if he were perplexed then a hollow chirping noise escaped him. "You were too far away from the village, and Darla says she hasn't seen you in a month."

The creature hooted, as if trying to speak but unable to form the words.

"Ah, none of your excuses."

Joseph smothered a laugh at how similar they resembled a mother and child.

Ashby let out a short whistle, catching the creature's attention. Robin jumped off James' back, barreling into Ashby, who crouched and held out an arm for the monkey's ease of access. Robin cradled the man's arm then leapt onto Ashby's shoulders, but reached for Joseph's hair, a glint of curiosity in his gaze.

Joseph raised a finger for the monkey to hold, like an infant. Thankfully, the monkey didn't bite him, curling his small fingers around Joseph's.

James breathed out heavily. "Let's go see what we're up against."

It took a couple hours to walk to the side of the island where the strangers camped.

Men of all ages and shades filled the beach, setting up tents and building fires. They weren't soldiers, unorganized in their different types of clothing and mannerisms. Camp sounds filled the salty air, metal stakes being pounded into the ground, piles of wood being chopped and staked, groups of men smiling and laughing together.

They each possessed a cutlass strapped to their hips and a pistol on the opposite side. Though many of them harbored other various weaponry, those two seemed to be the standard.

Joseph looked over the swords with disgust. Some of them were made out of cheap materials, like the pirates he'd encountered at the raid. There were quite a few made by his father before the restrictions on his work were in place.

Bottles of rum were tossed about the camp, the men drinking down the liquid like it was the life blood they survived on.

Filthy pirates.

And here they were, three men, standing in the way of a crew of ruthless raiders.

Joseph glanced at his companions to see James's eyes narrowing, but he wasn't looking at the pirates on the beach. He was staring off the coast. Joseph tracked his line of sight to see a ship anchored in the distance. It was a beautiful vessel with lilac sails.

Macha's Demise.

Seeing it in the heat of battle was different than seeing it peacefully float above the shallow island waters. The color of the sails reflected in the water below, making it look like Macha's moon was reflecting there in the midday sun.

The Goddess ship had been stolen from Samsara nearly a decade ago. Some believed it to be at the bottom of the ocean after it had sailed off into a raging storm. Evidently, that wasn't true.

Joseph's eyes tracked the pirates again, landing on one man in particular. He exuded confidence and authority. Every one of his crew members left room for him, paid attention, but didn't linger. A dark air surrounded the man in a cloud of smoke, as if he were smoking multiple pipes at once. His coat smoldered with little sparks of embers like the cooling rocks of lava that came from the volcano.

The rumors were true.

Captain Pike had magic. It was said he was a witch's son and had learned their craft himself.

Ashby's face paled, arriving at the same realization as Joseph had. This is what they were up against.

"We're going to die," Joseph whispered and Ashby held no objections. At his uncharacteristic silence, they glanced at James to find an empty space behind the log.

"*Mierda*," Ashby swore. They both looked around frantically for their lost companion, coming up empty handed. "I'm going to kill him."

"Unless Pike beats you to it."

A growl rolled from Ashby as he scanned the pirates on the shore, an ominous foreboding settling in his eyes. Whatever James was up to, they were about to find out.

A pirate jumped up from his log, shouting, "You little beast, give that back!" An answering chirp told the other pirates precisely what had attacked him.

"Ow," another pirate shouted, reaching for the pesky creature. He jumped back, grasping his wrist where red stained his hand. "The little bugger bit me."

"Leave it alone then," another pirate chimed.

A rattle followed, then their entire barrel tipped over to the sand, spreading bottles and fruits to the beach. The pirates shouted in protest, causing Robin to shout back at them.

"That's it," the first pirate said. "Come here, you overgrown rat!" The pirates pounced, six of them committing to the retrieval.

Joseph stifled a laugh as the monkey outran them time and again, but kept coming back to irritate them more. He would stop and dance on the sand to taunt them until they came in reach, then bounded off again.

"What's this?" Captain Pike finally took notice of the chaos and every pirate froze at his attention. "Who's disturbing my peace?" The men were as silent as a grave, smoke filling the air around them.

The monkey was nowhere to be seen, as if he had sensed the danger.

Behind the Captain, that girl emerged, the one with his father's sword. It was strapped to her hip, standing out amongst the dirty pirates with how clean and well-kept it was. She really was beautiful. If Joseph wasn't so angry about her thievery, he might have appreciated the way her long ebony hair coiled around her face, and down her shoulders, dusting her back. Or her luscious figure that was highlighted by the belt at her waist. Or the way her dark eyes reflected a cool gaze; one of stone and indifference.

Slowly, Pike drew the cutlass from his side, a beautifully crafted weapon with gold lining the hilt and a black blade. There was something surreal about seeing smoke curling around the captain with his weapon drawn and his punishing gaze; like a storybook villain come to life.

"If someone doesn't speak," he started, inching toward the six pirates. "I will not remain *civil* much longer." Devastatingly slowly, he lifted his blade to the nearest man. It was the man who'd been bitten by the monkey. He visibly shivered, babbling incoherently.

"Hold still." Pike grazed the blade against the man's stubble, giving him a shave that was unbearably tense. He inspected his work, as if he cared about the state of the pirate's beard, until he moved too sharply, leaving a trail of red along the crewman's cheek.

Pike grunted as if the red offended his careful work, but moved to the next pirate.

The girl stood stoically, watching her captain without so much as a hint of sympathy.

An impatient frown spread across Pike's face.

"Why is no one explaining?" He sliced his weapon faster than they could prepare for. Another pirate gripped his throat as blood pooled in his hands. The cut wasn't deep enough to penetrate his windpipe, because the man remained standing, holding his oozing wound, but still unwilling to talk.

Pike turned to the third man, the blood of his crewmen dripping from the blade.

"Wait," a pirate blurted, halting the captain's blade before it could strike.

"I'm waiting," Pike grumbled, his blade aimed at the pirate's gut.

He let out a shaky breath. "There was a monkey. It stole from us, so we were trying to catch it."

Pike's brow rose. "You mean to tell me, there was a small rodent disturbing my peace and not a single one of you thought to shoot it down?" The air changed again like right before a thunderstorm. Pike's nose rose in disgust as he glared at the pirates.

He sheathed his bloodied sword, reaching for the opposite side of his belt. The crewmen stiffened with the movement, as if whatever he meant to reach for was far worse than a blade.

The girl flinched. It was so subtle, no one else caught the small movement, but Joseph did.

Interesting.

Pike grunted and the crew relaxed when his hand came back empty.

The captain turned away, but the crewman spoke. "You're not going to kill me?"

A breathy chuckle escaped Pike. "My order was for my men to speak." He pointed to the first two men. "They stayed silent, they disobeyed. I don't punish the messenger. I punish the disobedient. A lesson—" he said, tipping his head to the remaining two pirates who hadn't spoken, "you would do well to remember."

The relief he witnessed in the crew's eyes told Joseph this was Pike in a good mood.

A low whistle echoed from behind them and they turned to see James with his arms crossed, leaned against a rock, the monkey standing on his shoulders. He was far enough away, the whistle discreet enough that the pirates didn't notice.

Quietly, Joseph and Ashby joined their friend, the three of them sneaking away before speaking.

"What do you think you're doing, James?" Ashby whisper-shouted.

A smile curved his lips as he pulled a tome from the waistband of his trousers. "Gentlemen," he purred. In his hand, he held a book with a rune the shape of a sun carved into its leather face. "Allow me to introduce you to the grimoire of Captain Pike himself." The monkey howled, as if the book itself forced it out of him.

CHAPTER 7

WHY IS THE BOOK GONE?

"Insolent fools! Idiotic gang of bilge-sucking scoundrels!"

Pike had been screaming for an hour, barrels tossed to the ground, bottles of rum shattered. When he'd discovered that his grimoire was missing, he'd lost it entirely. Luckily everyone had steered clear from him, but Angelica wondered how long that would last.

Mutiny wasn't something Pike usually worried about. The crew told ghost stories of what their captain could do. Some were eye-witness accounts, others were guesses as to what some of his tattoos indicated. The grimoire made him too fearsome for betrayal.

But now that it was gone—

Angelica held back a smile. She might have seen that officer nab the grimoire whilst the crew was occupied. He was a handsome man with deep blue eyes that looked straight into her soul when his sticky fingers had locked onto the leather bound tome. She witnessed the panic that had sharpen his features as they locked eyes, until she had looked away.

It was like an answered prayer. With the bloody grimoire gone, she could finally escape.

The whispers gathered around her, drawing her attention back to the present.

"Why can't he just get it back?"

"I'd not consider a bunch of women and children to be threats to the Captain."

She was close enough to hear them, but they were far enough away from Pike to be ignored. Though she knew he felt their stares. There was one reason he could not go after the book himself. One he kept secret from his own crew, for good reason.

She knew of his weakness because of her mother, but was he paranoid enough to keep it from his first mate?

Guyus fearlessly approached Pike. "It's a village with no one to protect them. We sail the ship around and take it back before supper."

That answers that. All his life, Pike hadn't told anyone but a bed fellow when he was young. This, she could use.

Angelica went to her father's side, risking his wrath, but he wanted to hear what she had to say.

"Captain, let *me* retrieve the grimoire. The monkey's interference earlier was clearly a distraction. I will do the same." Pike's attention turned to her, and she knew she had a chance. "I'll send a few of the crew into the village, while I steal it back." And then, she'd burn it. She could already see its pages shriveling in flames.

He raised a pointed finger in her face, a grumble rolling from the back of his throat. "I wonder, daughter, can you do what's necessary to retrieve it? I won't care who gets in your way."

Angelica straightened her back. "I will."

Pike forcibly relaxed his frame, but his gaze traveled to the sword at her hip. He reached for the pommel, drawing the blade. She flinched backward, reacting to the malice in his eyes. He held the sword in the air between them.

"It's a fine blade. I'd be curious to find out how well it cuts through flesh." His eyes roamed to the side where Palden sat on the railing, eating another apple he was not supposed to. Old Rob snatching it from his greedy mouth.

She sucked in a breath, seeing red dripping from his eyes. She blinked away the mix of the past and the present, but it didn't stop the ache in her gut.

When she was twelve, she attempted to escape her father. She failed, and it cost a kind witch and her family their lives.

Angelica's eyes caught on the little dot on her father's hand. The spell he had used to find her that night.

But, he didn't have his grimoire now.

"There's something poetic about ending a life on a blade meant to protect them." Her heart stuttered in her chest. "You best bring that book back to me, child." Pike walked away with the cutlass still in his hand, stopping for a moment to admire it before continuing on.

She wouldn't be bringing it back.

CHAPTER 8

THREE ANSWERS, NO SOLUTIONS

They sat in an abandoned hut in a circle, with the grimoire placed in the middle. It had been several minutes as they stared at the legendary book.

James had opened it and determined its pages to be unreadable. It was written in some long dead ancient language; if it even was a language. The symbols didn't seem to be something a human mind was capable of, but if that was so, how was Pike able to wield it? Did his witch blood give him that power somehow?

Whatever the case, it was clear the grimoire would be of no use to them.

But to Joseph... It might just be the perfect bargaining chip to get his father's sword back.

"We should burn it." James' eyes snapped to Ashby, who glared at the book like it personally offended him. But Ashby continued, "It's evil, and even if we could change that somehow, we can't read it nor let it fall back into Pike's hands."

James had a finger to his lips, seemingly contemplative. "No."

"What do you mean, no? We can't use it and the one person who can is an enemy who will gladly use it against us. With any luck, the foul man's soul is attached to it and he'll burn along with it."

Joseph couldn't quite believe the lieutenant would say such a thing. He was usually an advocate for less harmful means, though in a way it made sense. There was no detectable goodness to the man, and his single death could prevent countless others.

"I said, no." James pointed to the grimoire. "That book holds secrets we can't even fathom. If we can find someone we trust who can understand it, it's important to know what we are burning."

"Who would that possibly be?"

James leaned back against the hut wall, his arms closing around his torso. "I have a contact in Samsara."

Ashby huffed out a humorless laugh. "Why am I not surprised you're friends with a witch? It doesn't even matter. We are not *in* Samsara. We have no way to contact a witch, and a crew of blood-thirsty pirates are no doubt looking for the blasted thing. We have no choice, James."

Joseph piped in. "What if we traded it for the safety of the island?" *And for my father's sword,* he failed to add.

Ashby shook his head. "I don't exactly trust the word of a pirate."

James' gaze pinned him. "There is a myth, that if a servant of Nemain were to swear anything on this book, he'd be bound to it, unable to forsake his vow."

"So, we're believing in fairytales now?"

Joseph stared at the worn edges of the book. That instinct from before flared in him and he believed James.

Maybe it was everything he'd been taught about the death goddess as a child. Nemain wasn't inherently evil or cruel. More than anything she was fair.

"We live in a world where pirates appear out of thin air, and the dead walk among us." Joseph lifted his eyes to Ashby. "Is a magically bound grimoire so hard to believe?"

Ashby put a single hand over his face rubbing downwards. "That's a lot of faith to go on for the fate of an entire island."

"That's why I wanted to use it."

The three of them stared at each other a moment longer, the silence making it clear no one was budging in their opinions.

A resounding thud brought all their attention to the village beyond the tent. They jumped up fast, running to the entrance. "It seems we're out of time," Joseph remarked.

James stopped him at the entrance after Ashby barreled out. "Hide the book." It was a simple enough command; until he noticed the glint in James' blue gaze. This wasn't about hiding the book from the pirates. But from Ashby.

Joseph nodded. He didn't miss what an opportunity it was to be entrusted with it. He could see to the island's safety *and* the return of his sword.

Joseph arranged the book in his satchel, stepping out the back door of the hut. He kept close to the shadows, making sure no pirates spotted him as he peered around the wall of the hut, drawing his sword.

The courtyard had four armed pirates and a pile of rubble. It seemed the first thing the pirates wanted to do was destroy a statue. Macha's head had rolled far enough away to glare into Joseph's eyes.

"I think, by now, you can understand you're not welcome here." It was Ashby's firm voice, his naval uniform giving the pirates pause.

"Give us back the book, and we'll be on our way," the pirate who responded was a tall man with a triangular beard. He sauntered around the courtyard like he owned it.

"That's not how this works," James said, fearlessly stepping forward. "Perhaps, if I can talk to Pike himself, we can work something out."

The pirate smiled cruelly. "The hard way it is then." He snapped his fingers and a figure was dragged out to the courtyard, two pirates handling her by the arms. She was a feisty blonde who whipped and jerked in their arms.

"Take yer bloody 'ands off me!"

The moment she stopped, Joseph recognized her as the chief's wife, Darla. From what he had heard, they were newly married, not even a handful of months.

Roger stood beside James, his posture rigid as he took a step towards his wife. "Unhand her or I'll be cuttin' all of ya down myself."

The pirate laughed, reaching for Darla and seizing her by the chin. "I think we should have some fun with her first." She snarled, pulling her head back then jerking forward, snapping her jaws. The pirate narrowly missed losing a finger. "We'll have to put a muzzle on her first."

Darla actually growled. "Forget my husband. If any of ya be gettin' the idea of divin' into my oasis, I be drownin' ya there!"

The pirate arched his brows.

"Let her go, lads. You don't want to be doing this," Roger said, inching his way closer.

The pirate raised his sword to the chief. "Take another step, and I'll end her right here."

Roger froze.

Joseph watched the stand off intently, wondering if he should step out with the book. He'd save Darla's life, but wouldn't get a chance at his father's sword or getting the pirates off the island. He needed Pike to be present for that endeavor.

No, he could accomplish all three if he could get an audience with the captain.

Cool metal pressed against Joseph's neck, biting into the side of it.

"Hand it over and I'll let you leave with your life." It was a feminine voice, smooth and sultry. There was only one woman with the pirates that Joseph saw, but the blade against his flesh was too thin for his father's cutlass.

Joseph jerked out of reach, blocking her blow with his own sword.

He got a good look at the woman in question. She was a sight to behold. Warm skin, dark eyes, a frame befitting the Goddess of Life, and a glare so daring she must have thought the look alone would get her what she wanted. The sword in her hand was indeed a stolen officer's saber. He'd made it himself. He could tell by his initials near the hilt.

"Won't be necessary."

Her eyes narrowed further.

"How does a woman such as yourself end up with a band of pirates?"

She blinked, tilting her head. "Are you trying to get to know me? During a sword fight? I could kill you." She attacked, swinging at his legs, but he dodged.

"Of that, I have no doubt." Her technique was impeccable, the kind obtained by experience. She'd crossed blades with many before, but her form was lacking. She depended too much on her dominant leg. If he got on her left side, he'd have the advantage.

He rounded her, relaxing his position to make himself appear more confident.

"I'm still curious. Can't say I've met a woman like you before."

She offered a mock bow before lunging for his mid section. He dodged towards her blind spot. The opening was clear, her rib cage open for an easy target. He did not take it though.

She closed the opening swiftly, twisting as to not allow him the opportunity again.

"Forgive me, but how long have you been traveling with pirates? You fight like one of them, but you're not as cruel."

"Can a woman not be cruel?"

"No, the Goddesses are cruel on a daily basis." He pointed his sword at her in accusation. "But none of them would have passed up the opportunity to kill me while my back was turned if I had something they wanted. That's an awful lot of honor for a pirate."

A hollow laugh passed her lips and he suddenly wished for more. What would her real laugh sound like?

"Honor? You must be delusional if that's what you think this is."

His brows raised. "What would you call it then? Because it looked like you had the chance to take what you wanted and instead, you chose to battle me head on for it. You have more honor than most men in the Minister's Navy."

Her eyes heated, her sword raising. "Take that back."

Her little demand was... cute. Was he smiling?

"Stop that."

He grinned. "No."

She scoffed, swiping her sword to throw him off. There was no real aim to her strike other than to surprise him enough that he would stop smiling. How long had it been since he smiled? It felt unnatural, yet he couldn't stop.

The pirate girl's movement grew sloppier as his amusement irritated her further. He was even more curious now. What would she do if he irritated her even more?

Joseph used his sword to leverage the blade from her hands, throwing it far from her. She gasped as she watched the blade trail away from her.

When her eyes returned to him, he had an arm around her waist, pulling her into him until their lips met. He wasn't sure why he knew that was the perfect way to irritate her, but the way she tensed made him sure of it.

Distantly, he could hear the crashing of blades coming from nearby as his hands drifted over cool metal tucked into her waist belt.

Joseph could have sworn she relaxed into him, sinking into the kiss for a fraction of a second before her fist rammed into his gut. He grunted, stepping away and clutching his ribs. She had an impressive arm.

A hand swiped over her lips, wiping the taste of him from herself with a disgusted look on her face. Oh, but he got under her skin. He was sure of it, causing his smuggest smile to appear.

"What the bloody hell was that?"

"A distraction." He tucked the pistol he swiped off her into his belt. He hadn't planned to take it when he approached, but when his hand found the metal at her back, he acted.

Her eyes darkened, promising him a painful death. Somehow, he enjoyed the attention.

Joseph faced her with his sword pointed at her chest. He could drive it straight through. His second chance to kill her, but still, no fear showed on her face.

"Are you not afraid?"

"I've faced worse devils than you."

A pang of sympathy came from somewhere in his stomach. He hadn't even thought he could feel that way again. What was this woman doing? In a matter of minutes, she was making him feel a range of things he hadn't felt in years. Maybe he shouldn't have kissed her.

Before he could contemplate that further, she pulled a smaller knife from her sleeve, using it to force his blade from her chest. In the next second, she lunged for him. He dropped his sword in time to catch the hilt of her dagger before it plunged into his heart. Apparently, she wasn't completely unwilling to kill him.

He moved, forcing the blade from her hand. Gripping her wrists, he flipped her until her back was pressed against his front, her arms crossed over her chest.

"Let me go, or I'll scream."

"No, I don't think you will." He was rewarded by her silence. His guess was right, screaming would be as much as admitting defeat. She'd rather die by his hand than allow that. "Now tell me, who has my sword?"

She laughed. "Oh, you're the blacksmith I stole from? Pity. You've come all this way to be disappointed."

Joseph sighed heavily. "The way I see it, for you to be on that vessel, you must be important to the captain."

The pirate laughed, but it sounded even more hollow than before. "You'd be mistaken."

"I wonder how badly he wants you back."

Silence confirmed his suspicions. She was important to him. A mistress? A daughter? Likely the latter, though he wouldn't put it past the old pirate captain to take on a young mistress, he doubted that would warrant her passage on the ship.

But a daughter?

Good Davina, did she grow up on that ship?

She jerked, but he realized too late that it was her foot kicking away his sword. He searched for where it had gone, years of his father's training in his head warned him to never lose sight of it.

Her head snapped back, slamming into his nose— hard.

His grip loosened and she wiggled out of his arms, bending to retrieve the sword. He caught her wrist and pulled her back, but with a bleeding nose, he could hardly get a grip on her before she broke the hold with her other hand.

She twisted, running in the other direction. No sword laid that way and he deemed her to be no threat, until something hard hit his forehead. The object rolled to the ground, yellow and pinkish.

"Did you just throw an apple at me?"

She stood, resolute with a bushel of apples in her left arm and one ready to throw in her right. A tree stood behind her, providing her with a supply of ammo. He ducked before the hard fruit collided with him again.

"Stop!"

She did no such thing, another apple hitting him in the thigh. He ducked behind a boulder, the sound of apples pelting stone enough to keep him there. The nearby commotion stopped, followed by the apples.

Joseph looked over the rock to see the girl had gone. She was a magnificent creature, but did she have to throw so hard? He rose, one hand on his bleeding nose, the other rubbing his arm and leg where she had hit him, certain there would be bruises there soon enough.

The pirates were gone. The chief had been knocked to the ground, but he stirred, rising to a sitting position. James and Ashby were staring at each other, tension bracketing their bodies, quarreling again, Joseph assumed.

"What is it?"

"The pirates took Darla. They'll return her if we give him the book back."

Joseph put a protective hand over the satchel. That would give the pirates the leverage they needed. Who's to say they wouldn't burn the village down shortly after? Darla along with it.

"We're not going to do that, right?"

Roger rose quickly, barreling towards Joseph with an accusatory finger in the air. "That be my wife. I'll not be standin' here silent while you lot be decidin' her fate."

James put a firm hand on the man's shoulder. "Don't worry, Roger. We'll get her back."

Roger sent him an incredulous look. "How do you propose we be doin' that?"

James sneered, sending his eyes to Ashby. "I'm still working on it."

Joseph knew there was only one way. He needed an audience with the dreaded Captain Pike of *Macha's Demise*.

If that girl was who he thought she was, she could be the key to earning him that.

First, he needed to find her.

CHAPTER 9
ONLY A CHAT

It wasn't until Angelica was back at camp when she realized what Guyus had done. He'd ordered the pirates to steal the chief's wife. It was a dirty move, even for a pirate. She was surprised her father went along with it. He hated cheap tricks; he called them cowardly. Not to mention this was *her* mission and he had undermined it.

It seemed that the loss of his grimoire was enough to make Pike a coward, indeed.

Angelica moved the curtain aside, slipping into the tent where they held the chief's wife. She appeared to be a fiery blonde in a wench's dress. With an apron around her waist, Angelica didn't doubt that she worked at the village's tavern. She'd probably been subject to harassment by pirates and officers alike.

By the glint of defiance in her eyes, she had no intention of divulging whatever secrets the first mate attempted to pry from her. Guyus stood before her, crouching to be eye level. Her body was secured to a wooden chair with ropes.

"If you be thinkin' I have any intention of tellin' you a thing, you best be kickin' yourselves out the door."

Guyus smirked at her. "All I want to know is how many officers they left on the island. I doubt they decided to leave two behind. So how many?"

Angelica smiled to herself. They'd left three behind, but Guyus didn't need to know that. He hadn't come across the short, handsome man who'd chosen not to kill her— twice, now. Of course, she'd noticed the opportunity he'd missed; though he was right, she could have killed him the first time. So why were they both alive? Mutual respect? Angelica wasn't sure what to call it, but the same instinct she'd felt then kept her mouth shut now.

The woman spat on Guyus' face. "I'd rather be throwin' myself into Kheli's fiery belly than to be speakin' one word against my people."

Guyus growled, wiping his face. "That can be arranged." When the woman didn't reply, Guyus moved a hand along her thigh. "Although, it would not be my preference." Angelica bristled, wanting to cut his hand off at his suggestion, but she chalked up the feeling to one of pity for the woman.

Guyus took no reaction as an invitation, sliding his fingers further beneath her skirts, leaning forward.

Her head snapped forward with a roar, crashing against his skull with enough force to have him reeling back. Angelica put a hand to her mouth to stop the laugh that wanted to roll out at Guyus' curses.

He held his forehead in his hands, scowling at the woman until he pinned his stare on Angelica.

"You think this is funny?"

Angelica dropped her hand away from her smile. "She's a small woman, Guyus, surely you aren't having trouble."

Guyus nursed his head. "Then you take care of her, if you think you can handle the hellcat."

Angelica lifted her brows. "Does my father's first mate give up so easily? Maybe he was wrong about you."

Guyus stormed out, a couple loyal pirates following behind him.

If he chose to tell her father, she'd be punished, but it was worth the look on his face.

And then— they were alone.

The woman glowered at her. Angelica felt a wave of respect for her. She had expected pleading, begging, or even bribery for a chance at escape. But she straightened her back, not daring to underestimate the only woman aboard *Macha's Demise.*

Smart woman. "I won't be givin' anyone up, ya hear? Not for myself, or anyone." Somehow Angelica doubted that, but it wasn't her darling chief that would get her to break. Though, she had yet to find the right pressure point. All tactics she learned from her father, but that wasn't her aim here.

Angelica pulled up a chair, sitting and leaning back. "What's your name?"

"Darla. Remember it as the name of the lass that be stealin' the life from ya." The accent made it truly hard to fear the woman, but if it came to a fight, she had no doubt, Darla would put up a good one.

"I don't need you to tell me what I already know. There are three officers currently on the island. No match for all of us."

The fight simmered out of Darla's eyes, the bright blue easier to see without her eyes so narrowed.

"Why not you be tellin' them that?"

Angelica crossed her arms, relaxing in a creaky wood chair. "I don't *want* them to know that." Hope sparked in the woman's eyes. "Yet." It deflated just as fast. "Information is worth more than gold among pirates, Darla. I haven't decided how I will use it yet." Especially, after the stunt Guyus had pulled, but there was no better time to run.

"What ya be wantin' from me then?" Darla sized her up, maybe for the first time, trying to gather clues from her appearance.

Angelica shrugged, the picture of boredom. "Not much. Tell me about the island."

Darla raised one brow. "Ya be wantin' a tour?"

Angelica leaned forward, lowering her voice. "You've been very careful about how you fought the men on the way here. And you turned green when they dragged you past the fish barrels. Now, why does a fierce woman who lives beside the ocean get sick at the scent of fish? Or protect her stomach in a fight?"

Darla's eyes widened, fear glazing them over for the first time since boarding the ship.

Pressure. Point.

"Ya cannot be sharin' that with Pike."

Angelica ignored the plea that finally came. "Why not give them everything they want? Why risk the beating and the possible death of your child? Especially for information they would uncover soon."

"What do ya think ya fearless leader would do with the possibility of the chief's first born?" Darla shook her head. "These men be too close to beasts of the jungle."

Angelica pressed a finger to her lips, finding it too easy to slip into her father's way of thinking.

"Pike would eliminate a potential heir. He wants the island, but the value is in its people along with its resources. He doesn't have enough people to work the land and sail the seas." Wasn't he doing the same with Angelica and Guyus? Securing a legacy. She supposed the end of the world made that more important.

Angelica eyed Darla. "But that doesn't answer my question."

Darla pulled against her restraints, but they were secure. Pirates weren't known to be considerate. "Pike be wantin' the people with the island, but that not be meanin' he would not be takin' the island and his bloody book anyway." Darla's eyes darkened with the fate she anticipated. "In that case, I and my child be makin' an early departure from this cruel world." A heaviness settled around them, choking the air. "My chance be makin' them believe there be more on that island than they can handle."

Angelica held up a finger in Darla's direction. "You're just trying to buy time." She leaned forward. "Which means there is something for us to fear, it just isn't ready yet."

The Navy was coming back.

Darla's jaw clamped shut, finally deciding silence was the best course of action. After all, she'd just told the enemy more than enough for action. Did she have some hope that Angelica would take pity on her and her child?

Angelica considered her for a moment. If she told Pike all this, he'd act, striking the village with all he had, destroying more than necessary. The image of a man with a handsome face came to mind. Did he still have the grimoire? If Angelica were the wagering type, she'd say he was on his way to Pike at this very moment, ready to trade it. Something she couldn't allow.

A plan settled in her mind. She turned back to Darla, her eyes growing as the fear of loss took hold. All of that bolster and ferocity was gone, leaving a desperate mother.

"As I said, tell me about the island." She inched closer, but not close enough to receive the same result as Guyus did.

Darla swallowed. "What you be wantin' to know?"

"If you were to hide, where would you go?"

Darla's eyes brightened, but she shook her head, dispelling the idea. "There be caves. Westside of the mount. It be dangerous terrain, but there be hundreds. It would take one a good long while to find a soul there."

Angelica nodded. That's precisely the information she needed. There were dark clouds on the horizon. If she could get to a cave before the storm hit, she could wait for the officers to arrive. Without the grimoire, Pike wouldn't risk attacking. She could stow away on a naval ship. Samsara would be easier to blend into than Kheli.

With any luck, she'd find that cheeky officer and burn the book before the storm even hit.

Angelica took another look at Darla. That grimoire was connected to her life now. Pike would kill her the moment the grimoire was destroyed, if the bastard survived it. Angelica could leave her with her secrets, she already had Palden to protect in this mess. She didn't need two more lives to worry about.

Angelica stood, walking to the tent opening, but she stopped.

That same instinct from before, the one that didn't let her kill the officer, reappeared. The bloody thing was going to get her killed, or perhaps she'd inherited more than her looks from her mother.

Angelica swore under her breath, turning back to Darla and pulling a blade from her belt, a small throwing knife she kept as a last resort. One of two. Darla flinched back until Angelica flipped the blade, putting the handle into Darla's tied hands.

"Hide that until nightfall. Bones will be on watch tonight. He's mute, so you can take him out before he can alert the rest of the crew." Angelica motioned to her knee, keeping her voice at a whisper. "His right knee has an old war injury, so if you get him close enough to kick it, you'll get him down before he leaves his post." She pointed to the other end of the tent, where there was no opening. "Slash open the back, if you go out the front, you'll trip over sleeping crew. There's nothing but jungle back there. And for your sake, don't get captured again."

Darla nodded, taking in every detail with wide eyes. "What interest holds ya to be helpin' me?"

Angelica sighed heavily. "You don't deserve to die."

Darla's face softened, as if seeing her for the first time. A look that made Angelica feel uncomfortably vulnerable.

Footsteps came from beyond the tent, making Darla jump. By the time the tent flapped open, Angelica had her arms crossed, a stern look plastered to her face.

"Enough of this." It wasn't Guyus' voice that caused a chill to assault her spine. Pike hardly glanced at Darla, turning his smoldering gaze to Angelica, that tattoo on his neck seeming to simmer. "Did you get anything, daughter? Anything to redeem your failure?"

Darla gasped and the sound made Pike smile. Maybe she should have introduced herself to Darla.

Angelica let a cruel smile tip her lips. "Read her like a book, Captain."

Pike's shoulders physically relaxed. "I knew you had to have inherited something from me." Angelica bristled at the idea, but kept quiet. "Tell me, how many officers are on the island?"

"Three."

Darla mouth opened, betrayal painting her features.

Pike laughed, a deep and boisterous sound. "They think three officers is enough? We'll have the island before dawn."

That wouldn't do at all.

"But—" Angelica took the attention back before her father could spout orders, ignoring the pleading eyes from Darla. "I have reason to believe the third officer has the grimoire and has hidden away, planning to use it against you."

She watched the flicker of fear cross her father's face and reveled in it before he scoffed. "Child's play. He has no hope to use it—"

"And the rest of the fleet is coming."

Pike's gaze smoldered again. "What?"

"They sent for backup. Samsara's armada will be here within a few days."

Angelica watched the struggle take place on her father's face. He could take the armada if he had his grimoire back, if not, they would fail. It was a risk he couldn't take without the tome back in his grasp.

If he went after the book, he would risk swearing on the grimoire and potentially binding himself to a bargain. However, Angelica wasn't loyal to the grimoire.

"Let me go after the grimoire. I know who has it. I'll bring it back for you." This time, she wouldn't come back.

He pinned her with a glare. "Like you did last time? Guyus had to follow you to get this much done." Pike pointed down to Darla and she narrowly missed biting his finger off. "Take Guyus with you." Angelica swallowed her distaste at the idea, for so many reasons.

"I'll work better on my own, father."

"This isn't negotiable."

Of course, her father wouldn't trust her enough with this, but she took it regardless. For everything else, Pike played right into her hand.

Angelica nodded. "Yes, sir."

Pike leaned forward, searching her eyes. "Did our guest give you anything else?" She watched Darla tremble behind Pike, knowing Angelica gave Pike truths and lies to benefit herself. Darla's pregnancy would serve to keep doubt and attention off Angelica.

Selfish bastards were a predictable sort.

"Nothing." Angelica held her chin high, letting her father search her for lies but without his source of power close, he was less adept for it. Though a slight narrowing of his cool gaze had her doubting that. Was she about to lose everything to protect this woman?

He nodded. "Good work." Placing a hand on his daughter's shoulder, he leaned close until his foul breath ghosted over her ear. "Once we take the island, we'll celebrate with a wedding."

A wedding? Whos– A chill shot through her.

"It's about time I had a grandson, don't you think?"

Angelica didn't dare to let her fear show, but she didn't bother nodding as her father left the room again.

"I expect to have my grimoire back soon, Angelica."

She turned to see Guyus' eyes roaming over her. "I look forward to returning it to you, father."

Fear must have slipped past her mask because a self-satisfied smirk crawled up her would-be husband's face.

Perhaps, one day, she'd cut it off.

"Angelica!" Guyus' shouts drowned into the distance as she ran.

She'd lost him among the trees and could hear his shouting growing soft as ran the wrong way.

Angelica gave Palden similar instructions as she did Darla. He would escape in the night whilst they expected him to be sleeping in the crow's nest. He'd meet her in one of the caves and they would stow away on the naval ships together.

Now, she had to shake Guyus off, find the man with the grimoire, burn it and hope Pike died with it, find Palden and a cave, survive the storm, wait for the officers, and climb aboard without getting caught.

Easy.

Thunder rumbled distantly, reminding her that time was running out.

She reached the high ground; a small hill to give her direction. Though she stayed clear of the drop before her, the soggy ground threatened to give.

She squinted at the mountain before her where caves littered the cliffside. There were enough that Guyus couldn't search them all before the inevitable storm hit. It also made her chances of finding Palden impossible. They might have to survive the storm separately and meet afterwards.

A hollering call made her jump to the side where a hairy beast hung from a tree limb, staring her down like she was his next meal. It had black fur and a round face she might have once considered cute. Logically, she knew the creature was too small to be a real threat to her, but that didn't stop her heart from racing, or her throat from closing up. It especially didn't stop her hands from shaking.

Angelica reached for the pistol at her hip, but the monkey hollered at the movement, clearly understanding the threat. She moved her hand away and it quieted. She would have backed away from it had that not ended in her rolling down the hill. The little beast was blocking the way down.

"Look, just let me pass and we can leave each other alone." She might as well have been talking to herself, but her father spoke of the witch sons before. How the witches would turn their sons into animals to protect them. Though, she could hardly blame the fear around them when it was her father they used as an example of a witch's son who was not killed as a child.

Chances were that this was just a monkey, but on the off chance...

It turned its head, but showed no understanding of her words. Thunder rolled behind her. She was running out of time. She turned to watch lightning strike the mountain, rocks and rubble tumbling down the side. That didn't give her confidence to choose a cave there.

She turned back to the creature, but it jumped at her, its teeth bared and snapping at her. She flinched, taking a step back. The ground sank, until it gave way completely, and she plummeted down the hill.

CHAPTER 10

WHEN THE WINDS COME

Joseph should have known a storm was coming by the bend of the trees and the dark clouds rolling in, but he'd yet to adapt a sailor's instinct.

It wasn't until Robin climbed onto his shoulders, gripping him tightly that he realized what was happening. Distant thunder cracked in the distance, close, but far enough away that he had some time to find shelter before it hit.

He searched the rock formations near the mountain for any sign of a cave he could reside in and wait out the storm. It would severely upset his timeline of finding Pike and making him bend.

A grunt brought his attention to the left. In the distance, soft moans of pain echoed in the jungle. It was clearly human and female, but Robin clung to him like it was a monstrous beast.

Joseph pried the creature off, letting him cling to a tree instead.

"Shhh," Joseph soothed. "I'll check it out. Stay here." The monkey trembled on the tree, his tail wrapping around the trunk.

Joseph stalked into the foliage, one hand on the pommel of his sword.

Around a particularly large slope was the woman he met at the village. The one that had thrown apples at him. The last rays of sunlight shined on her through the trees as if the heavens were accentuating her beauty.

She sat nursing her side and ankle. The latter had a large gash, bleeding onto the jungle brush. He reckoned she had fallen from the top of the slope somehow, ripping her ankle open on the root, likely bruising her ribs as well.

He leaned against the tree rather than hiding behind it. She didn't even notice him.

"That's a pretty bad scratch."

Her attention whipped to him, a breathy laugh on her lips. "Well, if it isn't the sword obsessed officer. What do you want?"

Joseph hummed. "I have a name, you know."

"Don't know. Don't care."

"It's Joseph."

The pirate girl tried to stand, but her ankle was slow to cooperate. He flinched, watching her struggle to rise, that gash deeper than he suspected.

"Listen, Joe—"

"Joseph."

She glared at him. "I was out here to find you and the grimoire. But seeing as I'm in no shape for a fight, I'll have to see myself back to the ship." She turned, one hand on her side, the other holding her weight to a tree.

"Back to your father, you mean?"

She stilled.

Joseph's voice lowered. "I came out here to find you too." She nodded, pressing on with her wobbling until she lost her balance, falling to the ground again.

Joseph jumped off the tree, lunging for her as she rolled onto her back moaning. Before he could make it to her, her knife was out, pointed at him.

He put his hands up, retreating a step. "Not out of commission yet, are you?"

Her face tightened as if she was fighting back tears. "You will not take me back to my father! You can't make me go." Her head twisted and he recognized a desperation in her, one he had lost in himself long ago. Her hands trembled, the knife unsteady in her hand.

It would be too easy to disarm her. In her state, she didn't stand a chance, yet the spirit of the fight never left her eyes.

He took a step.

She flinched. "Stop right there."

He did no such thing. Instead, he drew his sword, and her breathing grew more rapid until he placed it in the dirt, abandoning it to the forest floor. She blinked, as if in a daze.

Joseph approached slowly, hands before him, as if he were trying not to scare a doe. Her breathing slowed, coming out in rhythmic pants. He crouched as he reached her, placing a hand on the wrist holding her knife, pressing it away. He didn't try to take it from her, only moved it to inspect her ankle.

It was in bad shape, a rock tore away the flesh at the inside, exposing a gaping wound with blood pouring down. The bleeding needed to be stopped.

He ripped a piece of his shirt off without saying a word. She didn't speak either as he haphazardly bandaged her wound. He wasn't exactly a healer, but the Navy trained him to patch up wounds with some efficiency.

With one last knot, he stood, reaching out a hand for her. "There, that will stop the bleeding. We will need to clean it soon, but we can't do it here."

She stared at his hand like it was poisoned. "Why help me? I don't have to be standing to use me against my father."

No, she didn't. But seeing as she was a pirate, he doubted she would understand.

"There's a storm coming. We best get inside soon."

Finally, she relented, taking his hand and his shoulder when he offered it. Joseph was hit with a wave of intensity at his decision as if this was a defining moment in his life. A thread pulled from Davina's loom.

He just hoped it wasn't a path that would take his life.

She leaned against him even if her face was twisted up in displeasure. Though he didn't mind so much. This didn't make them friends.

Robin came skittering out of the tree, sprinting for them. The pirate girl flinched beside him as Robin grabbed hold of Joseph's leg, the tail wrapping around his thigh like a python.

The girl jumped away, bracing herself on a nearby tree.

"Bloody hell," she shouted, trembling. "Wha— why do you have *that?*" Disdain dripped from her tone as she glared at the beastie.

Joseph lifted an eyebrow. "Have you truly never seen a monkey before?"

She took a long breath, calming herself. "I know it's a monkey, but why do you have it? I should've known the little rat was yours. Perfect distraction, wasn't it?" Was that fear on her face for a creature so small and harmless? But there was something else glinting in her eyes and he knew this wasn't just about the monkey.

"Still mad about that kiss, huh?"

A mischievous glint flashed over her eyes. "If that's what you call a kiss." Robin's eyes widened, as if the little creature understood the insult as clearly as he did. Her wrath then turned to Robin. "Take care of it or *I* will."

The monkey crawled onto Joseph's shoulders to chirp at her. If he didn't know any better, he'd say the little creature was actually speaking offensive words.

"I think you've made him angry."

She looked past Robin to glare at him. "I don't much care. I don't need either of you." She pushed herself from the tree, somehow finding her footing with a bad ankle. One arm braced her side while the other reached from one tree to the next, seeking out stability even as she crashed a shoulder into each one.

Joseph knew three things for certain.

First, that she was on the run, otherwise she would want to return to her father's ship.

Second, the storm was approaching fast, the wind shifting around them. She had to be looking for shelter if she wanted to survive.

Third, she was too injured to remain alone. She'd likely die before the storm let up. Which on Kheli, could last days.

"Are you following me?" She was panting, out of breath from her stubborn over exertion.

"Quite possibly." Joseph had secured his hands to his pockets as he strolled behind her like there wasn't a massive storm about to pour over them. Robin rested on his shoulder, clinging tightly, but blessedly quiet.

"I'm perfectly capable of taking care of myself." She reached for the next tree, nearly missing it and ending up in a bush of jungle foliage.

"Yes," he drawled, crossing his arms. "Yes, I can see that."

She ignored his tone, blowing a lock of hair from her face, but it determinately stayed in her line of vision. He had the strange and unfamiliar urge to brush it back for her.

"Well, thank you, for your help." She gestured to where part of his shirt braced her ankle, then plastered on a sickly sweet smile. "But if you don't mind terribly, I will be leaving your invigorating company." Robin chirped at her as if scolding her. "And the overgrown rat."

Robin howled, and she flinched. The monkey jumped off his shoulders to run into the jungle, akin to a boy storming off. Joseph hoped the creature found shelter.

Joseph sighed. "I don't know what you have against monkeys, but I know you won't survive on your own out here." He reached for her, intent to help her get to a cave faster.

She pulled her knife out before he could flinch away, pressing it to his neck. "Watch me."

He backed up with his hands in the air, but once he was far enough away, he smirked at her. "If you insist."

She lowered her knife, continuing on with her tree hobbling. And he continued on with his following. Of course, she glanced back a few times, but she no longer cared to point out the obvious. He wasn't going to leave her. The thought of letting her die, even by her own stubbornness, was unacceptable.

Eventually, she found a suitable cave, high enough to avoid flooding and with enough space to move further in, if needed. She seemed to hardly care, using the side of the cave to tumble inside. She lowered herself haphazardly to the ground, out of breath and a line of sweat beading on her forehead. He prayed to Davina that it was only her exhaustion, but he feared the worst.

"May I?" He pointed to her ankle where blood had seeped through the cloth. He wanted to clean in properly, but as she slid her foot away, glaring at him, he lost hope of such civilities.

Wordlessly, he turned around to search for firewood. Once the storm began, they would need the heat.

He piled tree limbs and kindling from around the cave's entrance, then went to work building a fire. She stared silently at him as he worked. Once he was satisfied with the burn and size of the flames, he stepped away to settle at the opposite side of the cave.

Joseph sat down, draping an arm over his knee. Then he stared back at her.

CHAPTER 11

WHAT CHOICE?

Angelica hugged her legs tighter, hunger pawing at her with grumbles.

It had been days since they'd made it to the cave, the storm winds at full force outside. Though she could hardly tell with darkness of the storm. It felt like eons.

She had yet to eat, sleeping only when necessary. Her water came from a coconut shell she found, its insides too rotten to eat, but, once carved, the shell itself still held rainwater adequately.

Trips to the entrance were getting harder. Her unwanted guest had offered to help, offered food, but she'd refused each time. She didn't want to owe him anything. It was bad enough she'd accepted part of his shirt and the warmth of the fire he built, but she didn't know what he would expect back for his kindness.

Likely, it involved keeping her healthy enough to trade her back to her father. She'd rather die.

There was no sign of Palden. For that, she was grateful. He could carry out the plan even if she failed, at least there would be someone who benefitted from her scheming. The boy was no match for the officer before her.

A pit grew in her stomach. She had no idea what she would do with herself now. Her plans became more foolish after being injured. The grimoire was so close. She had spied it in his satchel, exactly where it was the last time they'd met.

If he would fall asleep, she could burn the bloody thing in the fire. Apparently, he timed his naps well, or the Navy trained their men to live without sleep.

The irony of the grimoire being so close was not lost on her, but he was closer to it still. If she moved for it, he'd snatch it away.

His eyes narrowed on her, as if reading her thoughts.

The storm raged outside, branches swinging and falling to the jungle floor.

"Why did you run?"

After days of silence, she had to take a moment to register the words. They spent so much time staring at each other, she was beginning to think he would never speak.

She scoffed. "Does it matter?"

"I think it does."

She drew in a deep breath. She was too bored to fight the offer of conversation. "My father has mapped out my life. I'm his only child and apparently, a legacy is important to him."

Joseph's eyes narrowed. Was it pity on his face or anger? "Legacy? He wants you to have children?"

Angelica winced at the question. It sounded so innocent in the way he put it, like Pike was a doting father, excited to meet his grandchildren. Her chest ached, a pain that reminded her what she was missing.

She cleared her throat, refusing to let emotion cloud her thoughts. "Something like that."

"Sounds more like a slave owner than a father to me."

A joyless laugh left her, but it was satisfying to hear someone else say it, making her feel less insane.

"Who is it then, this potential father?" Angelica didn't humor herself into thinking his tone sounded jealous. The edge to his voice was drawn from the uncomfortable conversation.

"Guyus, my father's first mate. My father intends for us to be wed once he takes the island."

Joseph grew unnaturally still, likely thinking the worst. She didn't care for his pity. She held her arms tighter against herself, suddenly feeling much colder.

"Do you at least like the man?"

"I ran, didn't I?"

He nodded, his jaw clenching. His eyes lowered to where her hands trembled in her lap.

He stood, searching for something in his bag before walking over to her, dropping a piece of clothing in her lap. It was a light brown tunic, not very thick, but it was another layer.

She wanted to refuse, but he was already walking away and she was too cold to argue. She shed her coat, placing the shirt over her own before covering it with her coat again. The tunic spread warmth along her limbs. His bag had been sitting by the fire, warming its contents, including that bloody tome.

"What are you doing with extra clothing?"

Joseph kept his gaze on the flames before them. "I doubted the village would be very happy with me once they discovered what I took."

Her eyes drew back to the bag he carried and realized it was big enough to house extra supplies, along with the grimoire.

"If you take it, I will find you before you can reach Pike."

Angelica stared back at him, unfazed by his misinterpretation of her intentions. She would do everything in her power to keep it away from her father. Its absence was the reason she wasn't being dragged back to the ship now, through wind and rain.

"What if I don't want him to have it?"

He sat back down on his side of the cave, chewing on an apple he had in his pack. "I don't believe your own self-preservation comes second to him getting the book."

"You don't know me." Was it getting colder again? Her entire body felt like shivers were tearing her apart.

"You are a pirate, are you not?"

"Yes."

He nodded as if that was enough, but it wasn't.

A high-pitched howl echoed from inside the cave, followed by the patter of small feet. That creature leapt onto Joseph's lap, taking a bite of his apple. Joseph didn't seem to mind the beast stealing his food. In fact, an amused smile curved his face.

"Oh good, that thing is still here."

The monkey howled at her. It had repeatedly tried to chase her out of the cave, nearly working a couple times.

Joseph laughed, as he'd continued to do when the beast was irritating her. "He's not so bad." The creature looked up at him with what she could've sworn was adoration.

"You say that now." Angelica curled up into a tighter ball, her lungs pulling in the air greedily. "Once it attacks, you'll change your mind."

Joseph dropped the apple, letting the monkey dig into it fully.

"What happened to you that made you hate monkeys so much?"

She gritted her teeth. He should fear it.

That was the reason she said, "I was five years old when I woke to the sounds of them howling and my mother screaming."

Joseph leaned back against the cave wall, watching her intently.

"We lived in a little village in Moksha before it fell. There were many animals there, and they used to be peaceful, but the war changed things. Those beasts ripped her throat out before I could understand what was happening." The memory was so real that tears welled in her eyes, but she told herself they weren't tears of sadness but of anger.

Joseph's jaw clenched. "I'm sorry that happened to you." She flinched back. Even the damn monkey stopped eating, like it was listening to her story too. "How did you escape?"

"My father saved me. He's taken care of me since. I wouldn't be breathing if he hadn't been there." As much as she hated her father, when it came down to it, he protected and provided for her.

A chill racked her body, causing her to scoot closer to the fire. Why was it so cold? Kheli's storms were usually warm.

Joseph nodded, his expression giving nothing away, but she was thankful he didn't mention her tears as she hurriedly wiped them away. He studied her, maybe seeing her in a new light. She wasn't some fearsome pirate woman. She was a scared little girl with nowhere to go. The entire escape plan was foolhardy at best. Eventually, her father would find her.

Joseph's head tilted. "Are you sweating?" Angelica lifted her hand to her forehead, her fingers coming back damp. "You are."

Joseph jumped up, but she barely noticed, staring at her hand. How was she sweating when it was so cold?

He unraveled the cloth at her foot before she knew he was there. When had her guard come down?

"It's infected. Pretty severely, I'd gather. I knew I should've cleaned it." He pressed on the wound, blood and pus leaking from it and pain splicing through her leg like a fresh stab. "I apologize."

She tore her ankle away from him. "Just leave me alone. I'll handle it."

"On the contrary, this could kill you before the storm dissipates. I'll help you in any way I can, but if you don't let me, you will die." He studied her again. "Are you willing to die for your pride, pirate girl?"

She still hadn't told him her name. It probably didn't matter anyway. If Joseph had the grimoire *and* her, he had everything he needed to get what he wanted from Pike. But not if she was dead.

Angelica almost wanted to die, to spite them both.

Unfortunately, she had enough self-preservation instincts left to give in. She would have to escape him later when she was well enough to run. Hopefully, with the grimoire in ashes.

"Fine. I'll let you help me."

Was she beginning to see things or was he smiling?

The winds whipped and the trees bowed to the Goddess of Life, begging for Her to be merciful. All the Goddesses were cruel in their own ways and Macha was no different. She came in the form of these storms.

Angelica woke shivering against the cave wall, wishing for death. When had she fallen asleep?

The cave was empty. She was alone for the first time since the storm began. Looking around, she noticed his bag was gone. He decided to leave her for dead? Good riddance. At least she didn't have to go back to her father now, even if that meant cave walls would be the last thing she knew.

She shivered harder at the thought.

No, she would make it out of this. Somehow.

The monkey, of all things, ran into the cave shaking off its hair in the shelter. It screeched at her with high pitched sounds that hurt her ears. Angelica was convinced the creature hated her, though she had hardly given it a reason to like her.

She covered her ears. "Get out of here!" She threw a rock, but the monkey dodged.

"Hey," Joseph interrupted, appearing out of nowhere, completely soaked. "Easy there."

"Why? Were you wanting to adopt it?"

Joseph smiled like there was some humor to her words she wasn't aware of. Then she noticed the leaves in his hands.

"Were you a doctor in another life?"

He took the leaves, crushing them with a rock and a little rain water until it made a paste. "You have a lot of questions."

She narrowed her eyes at him. "And you don't have any answers," she shot back. "Or at least that you're willing to share."

He scooped the paste with his fingers and approached her. "Let me see your ankle."

Her instinct told her to defy him, but she was too weak. There wasn't really a point. At least he hadn't abandoned her. She let her ankle slide forward and he raised it to his lap, firelight flickering against one side of him.

"I was a blacksmith before I joined the Navy; as you know, since you were the reason I joined."

The reminder had her wanting to pull her leg back when he rubbed the paste along her wound. "Then how do you know you didn't slap poison on my open flesh?"

Without looking up, he said, "Robin showed me what to give you."

Angelica's jaw dropped as she looked over at the monkey who keened at its name. "You're telling me we're trusting the monkey with my life?"

"Yes."

"Sweet Davina," she swore, letting her head fall back against the cave wall.

"Right now, he's the best chance you've got."

Angelica closed her eyes, coming to terms with the idea of living again. If she survived, she had to face her father, unless she found some way to escape her handsome, yet inconvenient captor.

When she opened them, he was shedding layers.

She curled in on herself, pulling her knife out again.

He held out a hand like he did before. "It's alright. My clothes are soaked through, they need to dry. Close your eyes if it makes you uncomfortable."

Hesitantly, she closed her eyes, hating to have her guard down and not wanting another reason to like her captor. Like the broad shoulders she had leaned against for an all-too-brief moment before her pride and fear had interrupted. He may have been shorter than Guyus, but the hard muscle she had felt held nothing against his appearance.

"Okay, you can look now."

She pried her eyes open.

Sweet Davina.

He was wearing pants, dry ones he apparently had with him in the satchel, but his glorious chest was bare. She wasn't sure which Goddess she should thank for the sight before her. Every inch of him was hard muscle. His arms were built like trunks, the firelight highlighting and shadowing the plains of his chest and abdomen. His jawline looked like it was carved by Macha herself. His dark hair hung limply on his forehead, dripping from the rain.

She blew out a breath to steady herself.

"How did you end up like that anyway?"

Angelica took a moment to understand what he was asking, but she followed the path of his pointed finger to her injured ankle then her ribs, which hurt like hell, but she doubted the *monkey* had a solution for that.

"Long story."

He lifted an eyebrow. "I got time." He leaned against the wall, *her* side of the wall and too close for a stranger, but he was warm. His warmth seeped into her side, making her feel infinitely better than the fire before them. She had to stop herself from leaning into him.

"The short of it is that I ran away. I was getting my bearings when a vicious beast attacked me. I fell down the side of a hill. Obviously, you know how that ended."

He grunted, clearly resisting a smile, not believing her "vicious beast" claim, but not calling her on it either.

"That wasn't a very long story. Where will you go?"

Angelica almost laughed. He was about to use her for his own selfish gain and he wanted to hear what she would do had she been successful in achieving her freedom?

Selfish bastard. All the men she knew were, why would he be any different? As he had admitted, he'd joined the Navy and abandoned his life on Samsara to find her and the bloody sword.

She almost answered to see if he would show an ounce of sympathy, but she didn't want him to know more than he already did. "That's a cruel thing to ask a captive woman."

She didn't dare look at him, but she could feel his doubt. He knew there was something more but chose not to press.

Shivers, harder than before, racked her body, causing her to jolt.

"Lay down," he breathed.

"What?" A familiar fear pierced her veins, reminding her how weak she was.

"I can hear your teeth chattering. Let the fire warm your front. I've got your back." He said it dryly, like he was speaking to a fellow officer rather than the enemy. "Lay down."

"What about the monkey?" She eyed the creature in question, who tilted his head at her.

"I promise, this one is harmless."

"How do you know that?"

Joseph let out an irritated sigh. "He spends his nights with the villagers with no incidents. Now, lay down."

She obeyed, too tired to argue further, leaning on her good side where the hard rock didn't dig into her sensitive side. Her back was freezing. So cold, it negated what the fire could do for her. He shifted behind her, laying with her and pressing his front to her backside. They molded together easily, one arm curling under her head like a pillow while the other rested on her hip.

Sparks snapped in the fire, reflecting how her body felt in contact with his. He was careful not to touch anywhere that might hurt or scare her. She savored his warmth as it radiated through her body, allowing the fire to warm her other side, cocooned in a pocket of heat.

"What's your name?" He whispered into her ear, that warmth filling her too.

At this moment, nothing was wrong. Nothing could be. She was warm and safe. Her eyelids grew heavy.

"Angelica."

Sleep pulled at her edges, urging her under. Before she lost herself to it completely, she heard him whisper, "It's nice to meet you, Angelica."

CHAPTER 12

SELFISH BASTARDS

Joseph woke with the sun, Angelica still passed out beside him. Sometime in the night his arm had fallen over her waist, an action he failed to remember. He doubted she would be comfortable with that regardless of how many times she had scooted into his warmth like she would die without it. One by one he lifted his fingers from the softness at her stomach, until he was free to shift away without waking her.

As he stood, he stared down at her, not nearly so imposing when she was lost to her dreams. She truly was a sight to behold, her long lashes creating shadows on her cheeks from the newborn sunlight.

He was surprised to find she hadn't woken in the middle of the night to deliver the grimoire to her father. It was still in the satchel leaned against the opposing cave wall. She could have taken it and left him with nothing. With her current condition, she wouldn't have made it far, though he didn't put it past her to try.

It didn't escape him that she had run from her father on an island that gave her very little odds. Her chances ended with her starved, killed by the villagers or other island creatures, or returned to her father. And that was before she was injured.

Yet she'd still run. He wanted to both scream at her for being so reckless with her own life and smile at her determination.

He placed a hand on her forehead. Her fever had broken.

Far be it for him to trust a monkey with someone's health, but she had no other options. He couldn't stomach the idea of letting her die. He wasn't sure if he'd inherited his mother's kindness, or if the reason was more complex than that.

Joseph had a new fire going before Angelica woke. She stretched her arms above her head like a lounging street cat curled up in a patch of sunlight. The comparison made the very corner of his mouth twitch up.

"Good morning," she whispered with a groggy morning voice, clearly her situation had yet to return to her because he swore that was a content smile on her face.

"Good morning," he responded, enjoying the lightness in her eyes.

Suddenly, those ink pot eyes widened, and she straightened into a sitting position. Sunlight draped around her like a blanket making one thing painfully obvious. The storm was over.

She checked over her hands first, but for what, he didn't understand. Was she looking for restraints?

Before the question could be spoken, Robin ran up to her. She jolted, but didn't stand to run like she did so many times before.

Finally, she relaxed, letting him place the little apple in her lap. She had stubbornly rejected all the food he had offered her, but she couldn't reject it from his little hands.

Joseph smirked. Robin was intelligent. Enough to understand Joseph's instruction. He was beginning to develop a multitude of questions about the beastie.

"Thank you," she whispered to Robin. He preened in response, bouncing on his hind legs with his little hands on her thigh, waiting until she took a bite before scampering off.

"Yes," Joseph drawled. "Fearsome creatures."

She tutted, but didn't reply as she made quick work of the apple.

Once done, she turned to him. "Am I a prisoner?"

He had contemplated that very thought. She could be. Her infection was gone, but her injury was not. If he took her back to the village, they would exchange her for Darla.

His father's voice was in the back of his head begging him to use the situation. He had the grimoire and Pike's daughter. He could have his sword back and the pirates gone by nightfall.

"Don't," she whispered. His eyes snapped to her, searching the darkness there. "Don't give my father his grimoire. You can give him me, but he can't have it."

He raised a lone brow. "He'll burn the island down to get it back."

She nodded solemnly. "He'll do much worse if he gets his hands on this power again."

Joseph clasped his hands together crouching down until they were a breath away from one another.

"Then what do you propose I do?"

"Burn it."

Joseph must have heard her wrong. "What?"

"Burn it. Make sure the fire is hot enough to burn every word. Take it to the top of this bloody mountain and throw it in." Her gaze was intense enough to warrant his curiosity.

"What will happen if I do that?"

Angelica swallowed, her hair falling over her shoulder as she pierced him with her gaze. "I don't know." At Joseph's unconvinced face, Angelica spoke again. "It could kill him. It could explode the island with the amount of dark Goddess magic trapped in those pages. It could do nothing but burn. But there is one thing I know for certain, my father would never get his hands on it again."

Joseph doubted sacrificing the island to the wrath of a goddess was the answer.

"Whatever you have heard about my father, it's worse. He takes ships without looting them and leaves no survivors. The grimoire demands a price. Nemain always demands a price. The Goddess of

Death doesn't deal in treasure. She deals in souls. When he's scarce on power, who do you think he'll sacrifice first?"

Joseph blinked, holding up a single finger. "Let me get this straight, Pike gets his power from killing people?"

"Yes."

His eyebrows rose. "It shouldn't be a problem if I can convince him to leave us alone," he mumbled.

Her head tilted, studying him. "You know, don't you?"

Joseph didn't have to ask what she was referring to. It was the entire reason he was outside the village. "I know the stories. That Pike is bound to that damn book. If he swears on it, he's bound to honor his word."

He studied her reaction, but if she knew what the truth was, her face didn't give her away.

"And you're willing to risk your life on a story? I didn't really take you for a man of faith."

He narrowed his eyes, trying to decide if she was bluffing.

"If you would have asked me a week ago, I wouldn't be. But after being ambushed by his ship in the middle of the sea on a clear day and the smoldering coat thing, I'm willing to go on a little faith."

She nodded, an unreadable expression crossing her features. If he didn't know better, he'd call it defeat. "It won't work. He won't swear on the grimoire for anything, and that includes me."

He watched her face fall, seeing the acceptance taking its toll and dulling her brightness.

"The moment my father gets his grimoire back, he'll find me." Her breathing grew sharper as he recognized the panic in her dark eyes.

Instinct flared. He wanted to drag her to the village and hide her away, but the villagers would not allow her to stay if they could get Darla back.

But if she returned to Pike of her own free will, or if she managed to hide on the island, she had a chance at survival. Which left him with one choice.

"Go."

Angelica blinked at him, that brightness returning and damn him if she wasn't absolutely breathtaking. "What?"

"I will not take the decision from you. Pike may deal in prisoners, but I do not." She rose, finding her footing was a bit steadier. "Hide on the island or go back to Pike. The choice is yours."

Angelica stared unblinking, her mouth agape. He couldn't blame her, he wasn't certain why he was letting her go instead of taking her back to the village, consequences be damned. Except one obvious truth: it was the right thing to do.

Joseph leaned against the edge of the wall, waiting for her to leave, knowing she would. There was no reason for them to stay together any longer, although a foolish part of his heart wished she would stay.

"And you?" She stared at his satchel rather than him, disappointment flashing through him. "Will you trade the grimoire?"

"No," he barked on instinct. Then he remembered Darla and the rest of the island. "It's not that simple." A humorless smile lifted his face, but he barely felt it. "All I wanted was my father's sword back." She trapped him in her gaze and he held it. "Whatever happens, I won't allow him to have it back, but I cannot burn it before we make sure our people are safe."

Angelica drew back. "Davina isn't always so kind."

Joseph frowned. "I don't know about that." He couldn't explain it fully, but something about the hand of fate felt more real now. Things were changing. "I don't think Davina's done with either of us, Angelica." She finally blinked when he said her name, as if she had been waiting to hear it. "Thank you."

Her brows scrunched together. "For what?"

One corner of his mouth rose in a half-smile. "For making me realize there are far better things to fight for than a sword."

A part of him still screamed for the blade to be returned to him, but it was quieter than before. He still felt like he was betraying his father in some small way, but looking at the pirate girl, he knew what he wanted to fight for now.

He studied her one final time. "Be safe, Angelica."

Angelica stared back for a heartbeat. "You too," she said, hobbling to the entrance.

Joseph turned away, not wanting to know if she would even look back.

CHAPTER 13

FROM THE SEA

ngelica's ankle and ribs ached severely, but they were much more manageable. She picked up a fallen branch and used it as a staff, stepping through the tree line to see lilac sails.

It was clear there was only one decision for herself.

She had debated which was more cowardly, but had come to the conclusion they both were. In the end, she could die fighting or she could die shivering in some cave Joseph wasn't in. A different ache throbbed in her chest at the thought of never seeing him again.

He let her go, even if it was in his best interests not to. No one she'd ever met would have chosen to let her go. He didn't even demand payment for saving her life. Which he undoubtedly had, even against her protests.

Then he'd thanked her, like she had done the saving.

Her eyes searched the camp for the boy. If Palden made it out, then this was all worth it. She could make certain the grimoire was destroyed before running next time.

A pirate called out, though she barely heard it. She already felt her father's stare, impaling her from across the camp as the crewmen made it clear she had been spotted.

"Angelica?"

Guyus jumped up from his seat around the bonfire, the center-piece of their pitched tents. She held back a sneer at his approach. He was tall and overbearing, wrapping his arms around her like he could squeeze her into him. Or maybe he wanted to remind her he could crush her if he wished.

"I was so worried, *cariño*. I lost you in the jungle and you weren't responding to me."

Angelica breathed out a sigh of relief at knowing they didn't realize she ran. She had the storm to thank for that.

"I fell down a hill. I must have hit my head, because I passed out," she said, unwilling to disclose who exactly helped her. The half-truth half-lie was normal enough for her to get through without giving herself away. "I found a cave before the storm truly hit."

Pike had made his way over, his eyes checking her over. At first, a swell of warmth rushed over her at the thought of the concern in her eyes, but when his eyes snagged on her injury, she saw the distaste there.

"Get yer dirty hands off!"

Angelica tried to pull away, but Guyus' arm squeezed her like a python's death grip, her breath turning shallow at the lack of space. He breathed over the shell of her ear, his voice low. "If you ever make me look like a fool again, I will tell your father why you really left."

Her muscles seized up, her entire body on alert. "What?"

"I'm glad you came to your senses. There's no where you could go. You belong to us."

Angelica squirmed, trying to wriggle out of his hold, but Guyus held on tight. "Run again, Angelica. I won't be merciful a second time." It was an echo of what her father said the last time.

Finally, he released her and she regained full use of her lungs. She had more pressing things to worry about than Guyus. She may have returned, but she showed up empty-handed.

Angelica turned to Pike who fumed with rage. "I thought perhaps you had orchestrated the ordeal, but it seems you have more sense than that."

Her brows furrowed in confusion, her mask firmly back in place.

"That cabin boy helped the wench escape then took off himself." His fists reddened at his sides, but the smoke around his coat had faded, going too long without the nearness of his grimoire. "We brought her back, but the boy has disappeared."

Her heart seized, but a lie came out easily. "We'll find—"

Pike shook his head. "A mutinous cabin boy means little to me. We have an appointment to keep. I'm getting my grimoire back, and I'm not taking chances this time."

CHAPTER 14

FROM THE TREETOPS

Joseph stared at the grimoire, like the leather bound cover would give him the answers he needed. Somehow he needed to save Angelica, Darla, and the entire island without the tome ending back in Pike's hands. Perhaps he was beginning to agree with James to use its dark magic, but Angelica's warnings rang in his head.

He'd made his decision to head back, but as soon as he spotted huts and clotheslines, he stopped, doubt etching in. If they forced his hand and continued with the trade, Angelica would remain trapped.

He knew what her choice was, following her as far as he dared. Rage had nearly split him open when he watched the first mate wrap her in his arms like he had any right to touch her. Had they not been surrounded by pirates, Joseph would have ended the miserable soul's life for Angelica's sake.

"Can't change your mind again, mate." Joseph whirled to find James lounging in a tree, his booted legs propped up on an opposing trunk like he had all the time in the world. "At this point, it would be rude."

"I think caution shouldn't be overlooked when dealing with the fate of the island."

James frowned. "It's the island we're talking about now?" He swung his leg over and jumped off the trunk as if dismounting a steed.

Joseph straightened, not bothering to mention his selfish motivations. But he knew what he needed to do now as James approached him, one hand on the pommel of his sword, ready to win the grimoire back if necessary.

Joseph let out a breath then passed the book to him.

James' brows raised. "It's your bargaining chip, mate."

"I do have one condition. This book cannot end up back in Pike's hands."

A curious glint sparkled in James' eyes, the blue of them more striking than ever. "Is that so?"

"We need to use it to get Darla back, but we cannot allow him to regained his power."

James tilted his head. "Agreed, but that is certainly not the opinion you entered the jungle with. I'm curious. What other motivation could have cracked open that selfish heart of yours?"

Joseph felt selfish for most of his life, even if his mother's tireless teachings said otherwise. But for this. For her— it somehow felt more selfish to be selfless. He wasn't ready to come to terms with what that meant.

"Let's just say I'm going on a little faith."

One eyebrow shot up James' face, but he didn't question it further. "I do appreciate you. You saved me the trouble of coming after you, but we do have a rendezvous to attend."

"What?"

"Pike has agreed to meet for the trade." There was something to the tilt of James' smile that spread shivers throughout his body. "By the time the sun rises tomorrow, we'll be at the top of that mountain."

Joseph turned, watching smoke plume from the volcanic activity that awaited them there. "How did you expect to trade?"

James smiled, his gaze simmering with the cunning hidden there. "With the one thing Pike values above the grimoire, his life."

CHAPTER 15

WARM OR COLD

Pike's smoke had dissipated completely, leaving him entirely too human. Though his glower was intense enough to discourage the crew from taking advantage of his vulnerability.

Angelica avoided his path and gaze, anxiety thrumming in her veins at the thought of him seeing straight through her.

Her wounds were bound by the ship's surgeon, an old crusty fellow who she'd reluctantly trusted. It was either that or find those leaves again, but without that blasted monkey, she doubted she could. She needed her speed and strength if she were to keep up with the hoard of pirates trekking to the volcano.

Pike took up the front of the group, the crew giving him space. Over a dozen pirates followed behind him, two of which held an arm of Darla, her mouth gagged and her legs jerking, like she could manage to run.

If she managed that, they would catch her and break her legs. She didn't need them to be used in ransom.

Luckily, the woman was smart enough to not treat Angelica any differently, the secret between them safe, for now.

Angelica took up the rear with Guyus, who wouldn't leave her side for a second. Dread pooled in her gut at the thought of the trade taking place. The moment the book was back in Pike's hands, she would be right back where she started.

At least Palden got away. The phrase repeated in her mind as a comfort.

Though her injuries screamed at her for rest, she couldn't miss this. If there was any way to stop it from happening, she had to try. Though with Guyus hovering over her, she doubted she'd get the chance.

"You look worried, *cariño.*"

Angelica resisted the urge to scowl at him.

"Don't be. I doubt we will face more than a few officers on that mountain." Angelica's insides froze, but she didn't need to look at Guyus to know he was smirking. She could hear the smugness in his voice. There was something else going on. "After all, those reinforcements the wretched woman claimed would come couldn't have sailed during that storm. At worst, they are a day's sail from here. At best, Davina's Will is at the bottom of the ocean, all its inhabitants transferred to board Nemain's carriage."

Angelica's blood went cold. If they were going to meet Joseph and the other officers, they were going to be outnumbered five to one.

"Why are you telling me this?"

Guyus' hand wrapped around her arm, squeezing her close and halting her progress.

"In case you get any ideas about switching sides." Guyus' hot breath coasted over her neck and ear. "Just know, they think three of us will be coming. But the others will be laying in wait, ready to seize the opportunity to wipe them out." Angelica kept her mask on, not letting fear show on her face, but it wasn't her own escape she was worried about.

Guyus released her. "Just wanted you to know that. I look forward to our wedding night. With some luck, it will be tomorrow night."

Shivers crawled up her spine and she resisted the urge to tremble. He would not see her fear. He would not see her cower and he most certainly would not see her go quietly.

He tilted his head, watching her resolve settle.

"That's it, *cariño*. The sweetest prey is the hardest earned." He leaned in close enough to sniff her hair. Her hand jumped to the knife on her hip, ready to slice him open if he touched her. "You will be the most delicious yet."

Angelica wanted to throw up and plunge her dagger through his heart all at once. The stench of his breath was too close to bear.

Finally, he moved away, grinning as he turned to catch up with the others.

Angelica increased her pace. She would kill Guyus before he could truly get his hands on her, but she'd have to take her own life after that. Because her father's punishment would be a fate worse than death.

The fire crackled before her.

Angelica had already slept as much as she could with Guyus so close, but she'd managed to secure a different shift than him so she wouldn't have to endure him sleeping next to her.

When he woke her so he could sleep himself, she had hardly slept at all. Why would she? Any way she looked at her situation left her dead or broken. Neither of which she could tolerate. Or the idea of a certain officer dying.

She considered sneaking off to warn them, but she doubted the other officers would be as merciful. Though the blue-eyed one owed her for not giving him up when he stole the bloody book.

If she never heard the word "grimoire" in her life again, it would be too soon.

An apple rolled on the ground, stopping at her booted foot. She stared at it for a moment, inspecting the apple and the direction it came from. Out from the trees, a monkey pranced after it. The creature looked up at her with big understanding eyes and she knew it was Robin.

Robin tossed his little head towards the outcropping of trees he came from. Angelica had to blink to make sure she wasn't dreaming. The movement was entirely— human.

She would have dwelled on that fact had Robin not gestured for her to come. He was as quiet as possible, as if the little creature knew it would be seen.

Angelica moved to follow, checking her back for anyone who would see her.

"Where do you think you're going, missy?" A pirate spoke, one of Guyus' loyal followers.

"Can a lady not relieve herself?"

"A lady can, and when I see one, I'll point them out to ya." The pirate sagged with laughter, finding amusement in her situation.

"Very funny, Peter." She turned to walk away, Peter not bothering to stop her again. After all, she was the captain's daughter. Guyus knew not to trust her, but she doubted he'd told anyone yet. "I'll be back soon."

"Counting the seconds, lass," Peter called out, and Angelica doubted he could count longer than his own fingers could keep track of.

Robin peaked out from his hiding spot behind a tree, jumping onto Angelica's shoulders. She jerked, imagining his tiny teeth biting into her flesh and his nails scratching into her skin. She opened her eyes when his tail wrapped around her upper arm. He wasn't hurting her.

Robin's big tentative eyes looked at her like a lost puppy as she studied him. "Look Robin, can we make a deal? You perch on my shoulders all you like and you don't bite me." The monkey smiled then nodded his head and Angelica had to blink again. "Do we have an accord?"

Angelica reached her hand up, not expecting the monkey to take it, but he shook it like he was, in fact, human. Then he latched onto her hand, letting her help him to the ground.

Robin skittered away, tail high in the air.

"Okay, that would be a first," she whispered to herself.

"Now if I could get him to stop stealing my apples." Her heart leapt in her chest with the deep timbre of Joseph's voice. He stepped out of the shadows, still hidden enough by trees, but standing before her in his full officer uniform. It seemed they were taking this mission in style.

Angelica stepped forward, but stopped before flinging herself into his arms. This was no time to grow emotional attachments to dead men.

He flashed her a half smile that she somehow knew meant he missed her. Warmth flooded her cheeks. He smiled wider at the sight of it and she shook her head.

"What are you doing here?"

"I needed to see you." Her heart did an obscene flip in her chest. "It appears to be good that I did." His gaze tracked the movement of the pirates behind her, noting their numbers.

Angelica ran up to him, keeping her voice low. "You need to leave. If they find you Joseph, they'll kill you. The trade is a trap. Pike will get his grimoire back and he won't swear anything on it. Not with you outnumbered." She wanted to ramble on further and tell him what an idiot he was for coming here. How much danger they were truly in, but his dopey grin halted her. "What?"

"You're worried about me."

Her forehead crinkled. "That doesn't matter."

"Of course, it matters." Joseph reached out to her, wrapping an arm around her waist that was so warm, she could have melted into him. She hadn't even realized how cold she was before he touched her. "Come with me. We'll survive this and you can find your own life. Let me give you that." His eyes were pleading, as if he had been waiting for a sign that she just gave him.

She never thought it could be possible. All this time planning her escape and it was this easy? It couldn't be. Flashes of bleeding eyes crossed her vision. The fate of the last people who helped her escape.

"Joseph, I can't—"

With one arm around her waist, and the other on her cheek, he studied her face. His embrace felt so lovely, so warm, so safe, like she'd always imagined a home would feel like. A true home.

A single tear fell down her cheek and he leaned into her, kissing it away. Angelica felt like her heart was being ripped out of her chest. How could one man make her feel so much in so little time?

"Angelica? *Cariño?*" Guyus' voice snapped her from her reverie. She looked back to see him walking around the tree line, searching for her.

"You have to go," she whispered. Then she noticed the hard lines of Joseph's face.

"Is that him?"

"You have to go before he sees you," she whispered again, pushing at his unmovable chest. Finally, he budged, letting her push him into the shadows until he was out of sight. She was about to meet Guyus in the clearing, but he appeared before her.

"There you are. Peter told me you were taking a while. I thought I needed to check to be sure you didn't run again. After all, I did tell him to look out for you."

Mierda. She should have known he would wake Guyus up.

"Oh, I was just heading back."

Angelica tried to brush past him, but his arm shot out around her waist. All of the warmth that Joseph left her with escaped at Guyus' touch.

"What's the rush? I finally got you alone."

Fear spiked her blood, making her tremble. She avoided being alone with him so often on the ship that it nearly never happened—until now.

"Guyus," she intoned. "Let me go."

His mouth straightened, his entire body going rigid. He pushed her against a tree, one arm on the bark behind her, the other pressing so firmly into her stomach it made her want to lose her dinner. Or maybe that was his foul breath on her cheek.

"No, Guyus." She shoved his hand down, considering the consequences of burying her dagger in his side.

"You'll have me for the rest of our Davina-damned lives. Can you not allow me peace until then?"

"Why would I when you've never allowed me a moment's peace?"

Consequences be damned.

Angelica reached for her dagger, but her hand slapped against empty leather.

Guyus held her dagger in the hand she had shoved away. "Honestly, Angelica, being the daughter of a pirate captain, I would have assumed you'd put up more of a fight. I'm disappointed, really." Her throat closed up, her words getting lost as fear seized full control of her. She'd lost her means of protection.

He tossed the blade behind him, returning his hand to her stomach, then exploring further. She wanted to strip the skin from her bones in every place he touched.

A sharp whistle drew Guyus' attention away.

"That's not how you treat a lady."

Joseph stood there, a foot below where Guyus towered over him, but he did not cower.

"You're one of th—"

Joseph kicked him in the shin, something cracking from the impact. Guyus took in a sharp breath then bent over low enough for Joseph's fist to meet his face. One hit and Guyus fell to the ground with a thud.

"What are you doing? He's going to remember that."

Joseph's brows crashed down on his face. "I hope he does." He closed in on her, taking her chin in his gentle grip to check her face for injuries. The action was so caring, so sweet, her knees nearly buckled from beneath herself. "And you're welcome."

She blinked out of the fleeting moment, focusing on the man laying on the ground.

"I was handling myself just fine, thank you."

Angelica dipped to check his pulse, beating steadily. "Didn't look like that from where I was standing." She straightened, considering how she would return without raising suspicion. "You dropped this."

Joseph held her dagger, the handle towards her, his brows raising in some mix of cocky and shy.

"I have to get him back to camp without people coming after you."

All the shyness from his eyes dissipated. "Hold on, you're not actually thinking about going back with that bag of horse shit, are you?"

Angelica glared at him. "What do you suggest I do?"

Joseph was already pulling out a pistol. "You let me shoot him."

She put a hand on the barrel, lowering it to the ground. He rose one brow at her. "Yes, I'd love to be rid of him, but if I go back without him, it won't end well. My father already has reason to suspect me."

He moved the pistol to point towards the camp. "Why would you go back? Especially if your father would allow someone in his own crew to hurt you?"

"I have no illusions about who my father is, but when it comes down to it, he's the only one I can trust with my life."

He stood back, holstering his pistol and thinning his lips. "You're right. You have no reason to trust me." He held out his hand to help her to her feet. Instinctively she took it and fell back into his arms, his warmth returning to her. "Yet you somehow do."

She fell into his eyes there, wanting nothing more than to trust him. To find a life on the island or wherever he went. She could see it clearer than any other path. A hope she desperately tried to reject. If it wasn't real, and she let herself believe it could be—

"Listen, Angelica," he swallowed. "No one deserves to touch you without your permission. I'd love to end his miserable life, but since you've yet to desire it, I will allow him to live. But the moment his existence is worthless to you is the moment he dies. Because he cannot be allowed to continue."

Angelica stared at the fierce lines of his face. He meant every word. Maybe he was just a man looking for a fight, but he had chosen her. He wanted to fight for her. No one had ever made her feel that way.

Maybe she could trust this stranger.

"Let me see your blade."

"What?" Absentmindedly, she handed over her knife and he took it by the metal. Later, she would wonder why it was so easy to surrender her weapon to him.

Joseph pulled up his sleeve, sliding the knife across his skin. Panic thrummed in her veins at the sight of his blood. "What are you doing?"

"They need to see that you fought me off. This is proof. Blood that wasn't drawn from either of you."

"Well, you didn't have to cut yourself." She took her knife back, resisting the urge to drop it and stop his bleeding instead.

"Yes, I did. If we survive this, I want you to understand one thing."

He began walking away, blood trailing behind him. "And what's that?"

He turned to grin at her, his arm spreading to either side of him. "That you can trust me."

Angelica cursed herself as he disappeared in the trees. She was already in severe danger of that.

CHAPTER 16

A LESSON

Angelica couldn't believe they fell for it. When she screamed for help and the crew had found her with Guyus knocked out, they didn't question it. Not with the blood on her knife.

Pike ordered that the crew search the surrounding jungle, all the while Angelica prayed to Davina that Joseph had made it far enough away.

The doctor handed her a bowl of soup. "Eat, girl." She was convinced he thought she was still a thirteen-year-old girl. He was preferable company to many of the others though.

She set the bowl down, too nervous to put anything in her stomach. She was about to tell him so when she noticed Guyus waking from his mat, nursing his head. The story she'd told Peter should match what he witnessed, but she couldn't help but worry that he would be suspicious.

Though it seemed his pride was hurt worse.

Peter knelt beside the grown pouting man, whispering in his ear. Whatever Peter told him made his glower solidify. A feeling in the pit of her stomach told her it wasn't good.

Angelica stood, her hands flexing in and out. Guyus walked on the opposite side of the campfire, closer to Pike than her. He leaned down to whisper in the captain's ear and his father's eyes locked with hers just as fast.

She should have run with Joseph.

He blinked at her as she stood, facing her father as he glared at her. Angelica lifted her chin, meeting her father halfway. Pike nodded to two nearby pirates and they responded instantaneously, seizing her arms.

"Tie her to the tree," Guyus ordered. When Pike didn't object to the order, they carried it out, using rope to tie her to the nearest tree, the bark scratching against her skin.

"You ungrateful child," he snapped, extending his hand like he wished to strangle her with it. "If you were not my blood, I'd make an example of you now." Pike bared his teeth, showing the brown of ill care. "I take you in. I keep you safe. I let you choose for yourself, and this is what I have to show for it!" He raised his arms in the air, the other pirates looking confused. "She has chosen the enemy. How long have you been warming his bed, girl? Should I expect that bastard's child soon?"

Angelica kept her lips shut. It was too late to deny it.

"Answer me, girl!"

She flinched at the volume of his voice and cursed herself for showing weakness. "Yes, I had every opportunity to return it to you." It felt freeing, speaking honestly to her father. The rage in his eyes was both condemning and satisfying. "But I would burn every last page before I ever let you get your hands on it, again."

Pike's face reddened, his rage palpable, dangerous.

She would die. There was no way he would let such insolence survive. There was an odd sense of relief at the idea of her death. She could finally have peace.

Pike drew his sword, aiming the dazzling blade at her neck. One she was keenly aware belonged to the only man she cared about.

She could admit that in the face of death. She would bleed out from her throat, not even allowed to scream. There were worse ways to go.

"You must want to die to say such things," Pike said, his voice lethally low.

Angelica didn't respond, looking up at the sky as a tear fell down her face.

She heard her father grunt with the weight of the sword, but the pain never came. Instead, she heard as the blade landed on the ground beside her. But when she looked back, Pike had someone else in his grasp.

Palden.

His young eyes were wide, scared. He ran, just like she told him to, but it wasn't enough.

Old Rob, the bastard, smiled with one hand on Palden's shoulder, as if offering him up to the captain.

"No! Kill me, but leave him alone."

He squirmed against Pike's firm grasp. The captain held a blade up to the boy's throat. "Look in his eyes, Angelica. This is the consequence of betraying me. Your life still serves a purpose to me, but your traitorous actions will not go unpunished. Know that after today, the only thing that will change is your freedom. You *will* marry Guyus, and bear him as many children as you can handle."

Angelica's heart pounded in her chest, tears falling from her eyes as she looked at Palden. He was terrified, trembling in Pike's arms. He would die simply because she was a traitor. It wasn't fair.

A heartbeat passed, her father's gaze burning her. For a moment, she thought he wouldn't do it. The threat would be enough. It had to be.

Pike's knife swiped across Palden's neck, blood shooting from him, running down his shirt and splashing to the grass below. She wanted to scream, to riot, to kill everyone around her, but she couldn't find her voice and her hands were tied firmly behind her.

Palden's big brown eyes grew heavy until his body fell to the ground.

"Take comfort, my daughter. Soon your lover will join him."

CHAPTER 17
GIANT'S BONES

Joseph had thought he'd felt rage before.

Seeing Angelica forced against a tree by a man she expressly detested, awoke an anger in him he'd never felt before. It was like the rivers of lava flowing around him. Somehow contained enough to not harm, but if they were given an inch more of room, they would destroy everything in their path.

Bones lined the streams of lava, directing the molten rock in a safe path to the edge of the island. They were much larger than any man could grow, yet they resembled human limbs.

"Who were they?" Joseph whispered, not entirely expecting an answer.

"Giants," Ashby responded, glaring at the weathered white bones with a skeptical eye.

"Giants are real?"

Ashby let out a long breath. "They were, until they were hunted out of existence."

"Hunted?"

Ashby tossed his head to the river before them. The lava splashed against the bones; they didn't catch fire or even redden.

"Human bones have some resistance to heat, being the last

thing in our bodies to turn to ash. Giants are the extreme version of humans in many ways. Draiocht tribes hunted them and used their bones for tasks such as this."

Joseph stared at the river. "What a cruel fate."

Ashby put a hand on his shoulder. "The human race is going extinct because Nemain has released her beasts upon us. Is that any better?"

Joseph could imagine the lives of the giants whose bones sat before him and how they were taken before their time so humans could use their bones to manipulate the flow of a volcano.

"Maybe we should consider why Nemain sought to punish us."

Joseph couldn't delve too deep into that idea before shouts drew his eyes to James. Apparently, he had chosen the spot for their rendezvous.

The three of them came to meet Pike, leaving Roger and the rest of the villagers behind. Roger took considerable convincing to remain, but the villagers needed his presence. His trust was a heavy burden, but one Joseph was determined not to fail. He would retrieve Darla, free Angelica, and somehow keep the bloody grimoire from Pike's hands.

It was not lost on him that his father's sword was no longer on his list of priorities.

James had a smile on his face when they finally arrived at his side.

"Did you find her?" James nodded at Ashby's question. "Will she help us?"

"Yes, she will."

Ashby's brows fell on his face, making him appear older. "Then where is she?"

James avoided their eyes for a moment. "She may have required more convincing than I anticipated."

"James—"

"She'll be here, brother."

Ashby sighed heavily like a mother over an unruly child.

"Am I to believe that our defense against over a dozen men is the three of us and maybe a woman?"

James and Ashby shared a heavy look, the later taking the opportunity to explain. "We set the rules of the game in the first place. He wasn't to bring more than two men. Now, he's cheated."

"So," James continued. "That means we can cheat too. It's anyone's game now."

Joseph's mind spun. "You wanted him to cheat?"

"Expected. It's in the nature of a pirate to rig the game. If Pike wasn't so focused on getting his grimoire back, he'd know the better strategy would have been to send his men to take the village while we're occupied. It's a shame he decided to bring them along."

It still made no sense though. They couldn't take all those men by themselves, even with one more body.

Ashby's voice interrupted his rising panic. "Here they come."

Three pirates trekked up the side of the mountain, dragging a tied and gagged woman along, Angelica absent among them. A wide river of lava laid between them. There was only one way across, a bone bridge in the center where steam and smoke rose around it. As the pirates inched closer, James gained control of the bridge, standing in the center of it without fear, but a book in one hand and a sword in the other.

Pike stopped ten paces away from the bridge, inspecting James with a calculated gaze.

"Are you the leader of this fool's game?" Pike inspected James. "You don't look like much."

James smiled and it felt like the world held its breath. "What does that say about you then? I wonder—" James lifted the grimoire over the side rail of bones, hovering over the splashing fire below. "What's to become of you without your precious power?"

Pike seized Darla's arm in a vice grip, holding a pistol to her temple. "We won't be finding out, today." Pike's eye drifted to Ashby and Joseph standing on the opposing rock formation. "Which of you do I have to blame for my daughter's betrayal?"

Joseph narrowed his eyes, but gave away nothing. Last he saw of Angelica, she was walking back to camp. If Pike wasn't certain, Joseph's reaction could be the confirmation he was looking for.

"Dats him!" The small man on Pike's left shouted. "I saw him fraternizing with Angelica, I did."

Pike's eyes landed on the bandaged cut on his forearm. Panic flared in Joseph's gut.

"Where is she?"

"She's a bit tied up at the moment," Guyus drawled, sporting a bruised eye.

"Your head feeling any better?" Joseph smirked, feeling none of the humor he pretended to.

"Keep smiling. I'll tell Angelica about how you begged for death."

Joseph drew his pistol, aiming it at the miserable bastard's head. "If you touch a single hair on her head, I'll be certain to cut off your legs so you can't run away as she tears you apart."

Guyus inclined his head, like his words were the chatter of mice.

Joseph didn't focus on the way his blood boiled hotter than the liquid fire around him or the fact that his voice was dangerously low. He focused on the three men before him, deciding which would die first.

The man who revealed her as a traitor.

The man who thought her body belonged to him.

Or the father who should have protected her.

"Enough," Pike spat. He seized Darla's arm, dragging her to the edge of the river. Her muffled shouts could be heard across the rocky terrain, and by her glare, Joseph would wager most of those were threats.

He leaned her over the edge, mirroring James' bluff.

"You want the hellcat back? Hand over the grimoire!"

James clenched his jaw, walking down the bone bridge until he reached the other side. Pike retreated from the lava, harshly pulling her back.

"Swear on this book now, that you will leave and never return to the island."

Joseph wanted to scream at him that the bastard needed to swear to give Angelica up too, but he knew James had no intention of giving it up. Instead, he moved slowly to the bone bridge, hoping no one else noticed. James was surrounded by enemies. He needed backup.

"Guyus!" Pike growled and he reacted immediately, the sound of a pistol cocking making the intention clear.

"I'll kill her, boy. Hand the grimoire over."

James sighed, then tossed the book, the giant leather-bound pages landing in Pike's open arms. His release let Darla go, who ran past James, all the way over the bone bridge. Ashby cut her restraints and she yanked her gag down.

"Lend me a weapon. I'll be tearin' their guts out."

Ashby nodded to Joseph and he understood, handing his pistol to her. "Can you shoot?"

"Well enough." She took the pistol, aiming for the man on Pike's left and taking him in the chest with one shot. The man's body fell to the ground with a resounding thud.

"That will do."

Pike and Guyus ducked from Darla's aim.

"Now!" Pike shouted, a mass of pirates cresting the edge of the formation, yelling with their swords in the air. They would be upon them in under a minute.

James hadn't run, aiming his sword for Pike's head.

Pike blocked the blow and Joseph noticed it wasn't his father's sword glinting in the sunlight.

"You think you can take me, boy? You will die here for nothing."

James had a sharp smile on his face. "And what will you die for, I wonder?"

Joseph made it over the bone bridge to be greeted by a sword. He blocked Guyus' attack, pushing him back. There was satisfaction with the man attacking him. Now, there was nothing stopping him from ending the bastard's life.

"You were lucky last time. But don't think you will be again. You're not even tall enough for a proper fight."

Joseph approached him, resolve in every step. "What's your excuse then?" He swung, aiming low. Guyus blocked, attempting to shove him back, but he stood his ground.

Ashby ran to cut down some of the approaching pirates, Darla a step behind him, shooting down as many as she could.

Joseph struck again, nearly taking Guyus to the ground with pure strength. But his foot swept out, his long legs giving him enough reach to take Joseph off balance.

Joseph collided with the black rock below him.

Guyus laughed. "I'll tell her how easy you were to kill."

CHAPTER 18

DON'T LOOK DOWN

Don't look down.

Angelica stared at the setting sun, avoiding the blood and gore haphazardly left on the jungle floor, and wondering where she'd gone wrong. Perhaps, if she had gone with Joseph, Palden would be alive and she'd at least had a chance at saving Joseph. Or it would have all happened in a different order.

She pulled at her bonds again, hoping she could somehow free herself, but pirates weren't merciful creatures. They had tied it so tightly, she wondered if the blood would ever return to her hands.

Davina's full moon was partially visible in the fading night, the Goddess of Fate mocking her with the idea that this was ever in her control. No matter what happened, or what she would have chosen, she would have always ended up right here, waiting for her life to end.

"Is this what you've chosen for me?" Angelica whispered, her will to live dwindling. "Every lesson I learned. Every plan I made. Every tribulation I have endured has meant nothing? A pointless life where my only use is to extend my father's line?"

Tears slipped down her cheeks, mourning for the boy she knew, the man who showed her that some men weren't bastards, and for herself; the girl who never had a goddess-damned choice.

"Answer me!" She shouted at the moon, the light of it growing stronger. "Am I really worth so little?" More tears painted her face, drawing trails through the dirt. "Is that all fate is? A torment for us mere humans. To know that when destiny comes around, we have no say in our deaths? No wonder Nemain defied you."

Don't look down.

She looked.

And it was like living the nightmare all over again. Palden's eyes hadn't fully closed, like he was still in there somewhere, but the emptiness was undeniable. His blood soaked into the dirt below, flies already buzzing around the corpse.

You've always had a choice.

She tried not to see Joseph bleeding out the same way.

You still have a choice.

She blinked away tears, looking around for the source of the voice. It was not her own. Nothing. No one. Was she losing herself too?

She wouldn't even be allowed to die properly. She would fade into the agendas of the men around her until Nemain took pity on her. On that day, there would be no more goodness left in the world. She would leave the world knowing she had served to make it darker.

Angelica hung her head, tears falling to the ground.

Davina's light reflected in Palden's blood, growing brighter. Angelica sniffed, willing to stop her tears so she could see more clearly.

Silver light, more luminescent than she'd ever seen before filled the space before her, covering Palden's body until it began to blind her. She snapped her eyes shut, accepting her punishment from the Goddess of Fate. She'd insulted a deity, but this was an acceptable end compared to the one awaiting her.

"Send me to Nemain then. I have no place here."

Oh child, your purpose has yet to begin.

The light seeped through her eyelids, threatening to blind her even with her eyes closed. Wind swept at her ankles, her hair whipping around her face, but still she kept her eyes shut.

Slowly, the ache in her ankle dissipated. She nearly forgot the wound was there until the pain disappeared.

You'll need that to run.

The moonlight faded and she snapped her eyes open, leaning down to inspect her ankle. She could rotate it, no pain, not even a lingering scar, but her binds were still firmly in place.

Angelica pulled at the bonds, but they were no looser than before. Her initial awe faded. What good did healing do for her if she was still stuck?

"I can't exactly run if I'm still bound to the bloody tree."

Davina didn't respond. It was crueler than doing nothing, giving her that kind of hope before taking it away.

A little chirp drew her attention, the darkness shielding the source, but she would have sworn she glimpsed a tail.

The rope around her wrist loosened, blood flowing back and tingling up her arm like a thousand fire ants. Angelica wiggled around, but the bonds were still too tight. Then she finally heard it. Chewing.

Angelica whipped her head to the side to see Robin munching on the rope, the fibers fraying beneath his little teeth. A humorless laugh left her.

"That's it! I'm sorry for every bad thing I ever called you." Robin cooed in response, but didn't stop chewing. Another bond came loose and she could feel her lungs filling to full capacity again. "Keep going." She glanced back at the moon as the sky turned brighter. She had been stuck to that tree for hours and she was miles behind the crew.

But now she could run.

"And hurry."

CHAPTER 19
TOOLS OF A KILLER

Joseph rolled out of the way before Guyus' sword came down upon him. He jumped to his feet before Guyus could advance again, blocking his attack and not letting his legs slip again.

They battled on, Joseph's breathing growing rapidly.

Guyus let his leg come out, but this time Joseph lifted his foot and caught it, throwing him off balance instead. He stumbled back. "Don't lose your footwork, Guyus. It may be the death of you."

Guyus grinned, showing off rotten teeth. "You know my name, but I haven't the pleasure of learning yours."

"And you never will." Joseph lunged, and their dance continued. It was taking too long. Ashby and Darla couldn't hold the others off much longer and James was still locked in battle.

They needed a miracle to get out of this alive.

"Hey!"

The entire battle froze, attention turning to a woman on a raised rock. She wore a huntress' leathers of brown with one end of her skirt tucked into her waistband. Behind her was the mouth of the volcano, contained by a giant's skull, lava flowing out of its mouth.

The woman held a bow with an arrow pointed directly at the captain.

Pike laughed. "I call your bluff. It won't be a woman who kills me."

"I wouldn't be so sure about that," James said, giving the man a wide berth.

James nodded at the woman and she let the arrow fly. Pike dodged, but the arrow took root, landing in Pike's shoulder.

"You missed!" He shouted as she drew another arrow.

"Did I?"

Pike winced, tearing at his shirt until half of it laid in pieces on the rock. Black ink covered his shoulder and arm in an array of disturbing images. Through the ink, his veins protruded, turning purple and spider webbing around them.

James cleared his throat drawing attention to himself. In his hand was a vial with a pearlescent white substance inside.

"You've been poisoned. Looks pretty nasty too. I'd say you have about five minutes until your heart gives out. Unless," he paused, flipping the vial in his hand, "you take this before then."

Pike snarled, his lips turning up. He looked James up and down, perhaps deciding if the cure was worth his pride.

Guyus lunged for Joseph again, but he blocked it just in time.

"Ah ah ah," James cooed. "If any of you raise a weapon to one of my men, I will toss this antidote into the volcano and your captain will die."

"Stand down," Pike hissed, and they reacted immediately, taking a step back.

A smile spread on James' face. "Now, drop your weapons."

"Do as he says," Pike bit out. The pirate hesitated, Guyus opening his mouth, but Pike beat him to it. "Now." Metal sang against rock as weapons of all types fell.

James laughed, almost giddy. "The power, I love it." He tossed the vial again like it didn't matter if it broke or not. But it did. Pike still held the grimoire, and Joseph wasn't letting him walk away with it.

Pike grumbled. "You have to be a real bastard to play with a man's life."

James sauntered closer, a hand to his chest in feigned offense. "Just for that, order your crew to return to the ship. And have one of your men relieve you of your weapons, too." Pike's jaw tightened, his fist balling at his side and closing tighter around his grimoire. "Time is of the essence, *Captain*."

"Return to the ship. Guyus, retrieve my effects."

"Captain—"

"You would do well to listen, boy," Pike seethed, the threat clear to his tone.

Guyus nodded once, doing as he was ordered, though he took his time, taking every knife and pistol from Pike's person. There was a moment that lasted too long and Joseph stepped forward.

"That's enough, move!"

Guyus glared at Joseph before marching off the volcanic plains, hands full of weapons and the rest of the crew in tow. Pike's angry snarl turned to James, his free hand balling at his side. "Are you the demon I've hunted? My destined killer?"

James' brows slammed down on his face. "Can't say I understand—*ah!*" James screamed, his hand bending back against the bone in an unnatural way. The vial fell from his fingers, but instead of breaking on the sharp rock, it floated in the air, shifting in the winds before flying into Pike's awaiting palm.

Joseph squinted to see blood dripping from his hand, the blood soaking into the pages of the book.

"Turns out, you're just a man."

Pike opened the vial, downing its contents then smashing the bottle to the rock.

James slowly recovered, his hand bending back to a normal position, his other hand holding his wrist to anchor the pain. "You're still without your crew."

A laugh bubbled out of Pike. "You think I need them now?"

An arrow loosed, zipping in the air to Pike. He caught it with his bloodied hand, snapping the wood in half and tossing away the pieces.

"Fool me once—"

Pike flicked his hand and the archer flew back, falling to the ground and not rising again. Darla rushed to help.

James drew his sword, aiming it at Pike once again, but Pike tossed the metal away from him before he could swing it. James' hand bent back again, this time making him scream louder.

Pike held the grimoire in his left hand with a possessive grip, blood dripping from the hand he waved in the air and bodies obeyed him. Joseph squinted to see the pages soaked through.

It was blood magic.

"It's the book!" Joseph shouted before the air was taken from his lungs. Still, he choked out, "Take... it... away... from him."

Ashby didn't need any more encouragement, using Pike's focus on Joseph to his advantage and coming at him from the opposite side.

Ashby jumped to tackle Pike to the ground, but before he could, Joseph's lungs filled with air.

No.

Ashby bounced off a solid force, falling to the ground at Pike's feet.

"You think that a measly crew of child soldiers is enough to defeat me?" The rock around Ashby liquified, swallowing the lieutenant before he could stand. His arms and legs were covered, locking them in place. From the screams, it was not painless.

Joseph ran as fast as his feet would carry him, locking his eyes on Pike. James joined him, ignoring his broken hand in favor of ending this. Pike's attention switched between them, as if deciding who to punish first. Pike raised his free hand, ready to inflict his next wave of dark magic, but a tugging drew his attention away.

Darla had snuck up behind Pike, attempting to pull the book from under his arm. "You've caused enough trouble."

"No," James shouted a moment before Darla's body went flying, the unnatural wind carrying her a few feet away. A sickening crunch and a scream sounded as she hit the ground.

Joseph ran to her aid, but she halted him with a single hand. "It only be me arm. Take him!"

James and Joseph turned to the captain, ire dripping from his malevolent eyes. "Ah, so it is my favorite two left. Good." Pike stomped on Ashby's stomach before stepping over him, the man groaning at the new injury. With the menacing smile curving Pike's lips, Joseph knew there would be worse in store for them.

He focused his gaze on James. "Let's see how you enjoy being toyed with."

The rocks shook around him, bending and swaying like waves until they focused on one singular body. A snake the size of a tree rose from the river of lava, molten rock dripping from its fangs.

"Well, that's a new one—" James snagged his fallen sword in his left hand, facing the snake. "Come on!" The snake snapped its jaws at him, James barely deflecting the blows with his sword.

"And you," Pike addressed, gaining Joseph's attention. "You are the worst one, turning my own *daughter* against me."

Pike's free hand lashed out, and it felt like he'd plunged it into Joseph's gut. His insides burned like scorching hot flames. Joseph ripped his shirt open, but there was nothing touching him, nothing penetrating his skin or making it red. There was Pike's dirty calloused hand and the pain.

There was no room in his mind to think, only the agony and a feeling of complete defeat.

He'd failed everyone. He'd failed his father for never retrieving the sword. He'd failed the island for not protecting them. He'd failed Roger for losing his wife. He'd failed *her*.

What was left to die for?

The fire spread, overtaking his senses so severely he felt like his eyes might melt.

Distantly, he heard Pike's full laughter. He had defeated them so swiftly.

Then the laughter stopped, but the heat didn't, and Joseph thought that perhaps he had entered Hell and the torment would continue eternally.

A soft voice drew him to reality.

"I won't let you hurt him."

CHAPTER 20

A BASTARD'S CHOICE

The old dusty book was in Angelica's hands, pages open to the spells Pike was using. She'd stolen it from under his arm while he was occupied hurting Joseph. She already knew his screams would live in her nightmares.

Angelica focused on the pages before her. She couldn't make out any words or images with all the blood, but she could see old stains upon the parchment beneath the wet crimson. Pike had spread his blood across four pages, granting him the powers he was using against them.

She tore the page before her. Her father was already after her, attempting to use his powers to take her down, but she felt little effect. She wasn't sure if it was her relation to him or the book protecting itself.

Pain laced her spine, but not enough to make her stumble. Pythons of rock slithering at her feet and struck, but continued to miss as she ran. She sprinted for that river of fire.

"Angelica, don't—"

She threw a page into the river, the edges burning before the entire parchment was consumed. Angelica felt the volcano move, a tremor in rebellion to the destruction of the sacred tome.

She searched for Joseph, his form fuzzy in the smoke and steam. Finally, the area cleared, allowing her to see him stand, breathing hard, but he wasn't screaming anymore.

"Angelica," her father called her attention back to him. He crept up to her, his hands out so as not to scare her away. Behind him, one of the officers battled a large rock snake, leading it away from three figures on the ground. One of which she recognized— Darla. She was wrapping a torn scrap of her dress around her arm.

"Look at me."

Angelica's eyes snapped to Pike's out of instinct, awakening that part of her that always wanted to please her father. That little girl who wanted to make her father proud, so she learned how to wield a blade.

"You don't have to do this. We can go back to the way things were; better, even."

Angelica's brows scrunched together. "What could you possibly give me that you have not already taken away?" Palden's face flashed before her eyes, reminding her of what he had taken and what it meant to love anyone. Her eyes wandered to Joseph, an ache making her chest throb.

Pike followed her gaze. "You want him? Done." He focused his hand and Joseph's body jolted forward, landing on his hands and knees in the space between Angelica and her father. Those deep knowing eyes of his locked with Angelica's. She knew her father's ways. This wasn't just a temptation. It was a threat.

"He could be yours, Angelica. You're the daughter of the most feared pirate in the Sumerian Sea. You can have anyone you want. You could rule this island." Finally, she looked back to her father. "I'd leave you to be their chief, the only person you'd have to answer to is me. Anything you want, it's yours."

"Don't do it—" Joseph's words were cut off as Pike silenced him. When he tried to stand, Pike forced him to the ground.

"Angelica. I'll swear on my life, on the grimoire, on Nemain herself if I must." Pike inched closer, extending his hand out. "Just give me the book and I'll give you anything you could ever ask for."

Angelica wanted to. She wanted what her father promised. She knew he would do it too. He'd give her the world for the book in her hands. Part of her wished he valued her as much as the bundle of old parchment in her hand. She'd even wondered why he'd bothered to save her all those years ago.

As her father got closer, she squinted at the ink marking his arm. She'd never really seen that picture before because he never took his shirt off. Branded across his arm was a monkey, but nothing like Robin's sweet curious eyes. His monkey was a rabid monster, foaming at the mouth and snarling. Memories assaulted her, monkeys with the same maddened expressions and an aggression that she hadn't seen since. They tore through her village, tearing her mother to shreds in the middle of the night.

Angelica blinked out of the memory, finally seeing the truth.

Anger rose quicker than the volcano behind them even could. Maybe he witnessed the rage in her eyes, because she swore fear flashed in his eyes.

She tore another bloody page. "This is for my mother." The page was burning before Pike could lunge for it. The ground moaned, Macha retaliating. Pike's face turned red and he advanced, but his steps were stopped short by Joseph, tugging him down by his ankle.

Parchment ripped beneath her fingertips. "This is for Palden." The rocks rolled beneath her feet as the third page burned, liquid fire spitting out of the giant's skull. Rocks fell back to the ground as the snake disappeared; an officer dusting pebbles off his uniform.

Pike kicked at Joseph's head, but he got his feet beneath him quicker, holding Pike steady to the ground.

There was one more page with blood on it. "This one is for me and the life you stole from me." The page dropped slower, Pike screaming as it burned and the last dregs of his power winked out.

The other two officers were on him before he could rise.

A look back confirmed Darla draped around the shoulders of

another woman, making their way off the rocky plain. The nameless woman stopped and nodded at her, with a 'thank you' she could feel in her bones. Then they left, disappearing over the edge of the hill.

Angelica narrowed her eyes on her father as she held the book over the river next.

"You burn that book; you destroy this entire island. Are you willing to sacrifice so many lives just to be rid of your father, including your own?"

It would be so simple to drop the book, letting it burn and allowing Nemain to carry them all home. But that death wasn't just hers and her father's. It was the three men before her, the two women running from the volcano's wrath, the pirate crew that deserved it and the villagers who did not. It even included the Samsarans who would starve from eliminating their food source.

But even with all that. It was looking into Joseph's eyes that made her stop. He didn't tell her what choice to make, but she could see it, the future they could have together. She could find happiness she hadn't known since she was five. She could have a family she would love and children who would know the love of both their parents.

Selfish bastards are a predictable sort.

She cradled the book to her chest, and an audible breath left Pike.

"What do we do with him?" The tallest of the three men bent to stand Pike up, but he flinched out of reach, a knife in his hand. Joseph inspected his pockets; Pike had lifted it off him.

"You mongrels have no decision over my fate. Only Davina knows the day." He backed away from them, before turning and running. Some fear Angelica had been harboring melted away at the sight of Pike running away.

"Well if no one else is willing," Joseph started, cocking his pistol back. No one spoke up to stop him. No one, but Macha herself.

The ground roared, blowing all four of them off balance. Joseph reached out to steady Angelica as they all turned to the mouth of the volcano. Lava poured from the giant's jaw, the force of it so strong, it was breaking free of its cage. The river overflowed its skeletal confinement, the rock cracking around it.

"It's time to go, mates," said the officer who had stolen the grimoire in the first place.

Joseph had an arm around Angelica's waist urging her forward.

All four of them ran as fast as their legs could carry them. They reached the edge of the rocky plain just as the giant's skull exploded, fire rushing after them. They jumped, meeting a steep hill.

Angelica hit the ground hard, rolling on her back and clutching the grimoire. If she left it behind and it burned, they were all dead anyway. She groaned at the impact that made her dizzy, cuts and bruises lining her arms.

Bits of flaming rock fell around her, catching the trees on fire.

It took a few more steps before the jungle was blazing around her.

Her legs screamed at her and her lungs heaved with the exertion and smoke, but Joseph ran beside her, keeping pace. They would make it out. They had to.

Angelica didn't need to turn around to know the fire was after them, she could feel the heat of it scorching her back. Little sparks snapped off blazing trees, burning her clothes, the back of her hand. Smoke rose all around them, making the air harder and harder to take in.

The other two officers sprinted in front of her. The black haired one shouted back, "You're going to need to jump."

"Again?" Joseph called out between pants.

"No time to argue." A clearing of trees came, the sky stretching out before them, and the sound of rushing water coming from the left. "Now!"

The two officers leapt, falling from a cliffside. Angelica knew she couldn't stop, her legs barreling her towards the point of no return.

But it was Joseph's hand locking with her free one that gave her the courage to jump.

CHAPTER 21
HUFGUFA

Hours later, Joseph watched from a cliffside near the sea as *Macha's Demise* waded out to sea.

They had landed in the lake, right beside a great waterfall. The body of water was enough to keep them safe. Macha was not angry enough to destroy the island completely. With the recent storm and flooding, much of the island was too damp to catch fire. The highest peaks paid the price.

Now, they watched the pirates sail away as the sea splashed twenty feet below them.

Angelica's hand trembled in his as she watched her father sail away. Was she scared of what this new future would hold for her? Or was she more afraid of what could happen if her old life came back to haunt her?

James had scarcely taken his eyes off the grimoire in his hands. Angelica had handed it off to him when he promised to keep it out of the reach of her father.

Ashby had scarcely taken his eyes off James, concern creasing the space between his brows.

A ship sailed in the distance, too far to make out properly, but there was one ship that would be headed their way. *Davina's Will* was coming to pick up the abandoned officers.

They'd force him to return or label him a deserter. An offense punishable by death. He couldn't remain on the island with Angelica, as much as it pained him. They'd drag him back to the Navy no matter what he chose.

Macha's Demise could come back while he was gone— No, not could. Would. Pike wouldn't let her go so easily.

"We've made a mistake," Joseph breathed, afraid to voice his fears, but knowing damn well they had to be said.

The pain on James's face confirmed his fears before he could voice them.

"I know."

"They'll be back," Angelica added, staring at her father's ship as it sailed.

"I know."

"They'll be ready," Joseph said, his rage at the idea burning his insides.

"I know."

"They'll take me," Angelica breathed.

"No, no. That's not going to happen." Joseph squeezed her hand hoping it would banish her fears, but what good could he do if the choice was leave or die.

"It's too late now," Ashby added. "They're gone."

Light brightened James' face as he stared at the grimoire in his hands. "No, it's not." He opened the book, flipping through the pages for something.

"What are you doing?" Ashby demanded.

"Making this island safe."

His hands stopped on a page that made Joseph's blood run cold. He held out a hand to Joseph. "Earhart, if you please," he prompted.

Joseph's hands moved of their own accord, instinctively knowing what James needed as blue glinted in his vision. He swiped a blade over James' palm, blood pooling there. James used his thumb to spread the blood over his palm before slamming it on the book.

"James, no, you can't do this." Ashby lunged to take the book from James, but it was as if a wind had blown him back. Apparently, the book didn't wish to be disturbed. "Listen to me, James. It is not worth your soul!"

"That ship has already sailed, brother," James murmured low enough that Ashby might not have heard, but Joseph did. He slipped an arm around Angelica's waist, pressing her close to his side.

James looked to Joseph and he nodded.

"Do it," he said, the wind feeling like it changed directions.

"*Hafgufa, conjuro te aeternum de profundo maris. Hafgufa, inicios tuos occidere.*"

The world held its breath as the final words were spoken. No birds. No wind. Not anything.

Until a wave going the wrong direction slammed into *Macha's Demise*. The men aboard shouted and scrambled as the ship rocked with the impact.

Joseph pulled out his scope, focusing on the ship. Pirates ran about the ship, trying to understand what was wrong. He spotted Pike looking over the side of the railing. Pike saw something beneath the waves, something that made his skin pale, then he lifted his gaze until it landed on them.

Joseph could have sworn there was a smile on his face. He moved the scope until he could see the side of the ship.

Tentacles the size of tree trucks slid across the hull. Angelica sucked in a breath; the arms of that beast large enough for her to spot now. Pirates backed up as the tentacles slid onto the ship like large snakes. Guyus lunged his sword at one, drawing blood, but not enough to slow the attack. The creature retaliated, wrapping a tentacle around the first mate and dragging him to the depths. Guyus screamed until he disappeared beneath the waves.

Pirates shouted as those tentacles attacked, pulling men to the ocean while others broke apart the sails and mast. The lilac sails tore into shreds beneath the weight of those enormous arms.

Gunfire and cannon fire sounded from the ship as the pirates put everything they had into keeping the beast away, but nothing seemed to work, the creature was resilient against their attacks.

Fins peppered the waves as sea creatures answered the call of blood. Sharks circled the monster and the ship, as if they knew what its presence would bring.

Any pirates who found themselves in the sea were quickly torn apart by hungry sharks, ripping their flesh apart and filling the waves with blood. It was the fate that awaited any pirate who abandoned ship.

Joseph roamed his eyes over the ship, looking for its captain. If Pike survived, this would all be for nothing.

Pike stood at the helm, looking off into the distance as if he was personally sailing the ship to Hell. Nemain's Carriage wasn't needed if Pike intended to sail the souls of his ship to the Goddess himself.

A booming crack echoed loud enough to silence the rest of the world. The mast cracked under the force of pressure, falling to the ship and taking the other sails along with it.

Angelica clutched Joseph's hand in a vice grip.

Two tentacles much larger than the others wrapped around the center of the ship, splitting it in two and damning the ship to the seas.

Pike sent them a final salute as *Macha's Demise* disappeared into the ocean, screams haunting the winds.

A chilly breeze passed over them and James groaned, falling to his knees. Joseph rushed to him. Maybe the magic was too much for him to handle. James had one hand on his neck, rubbing at his skin as black swirls appeared.

"What's happening?" Ashby demanded.

"The grimoire demands a price," Angelica spoke softly, something like pity darkening her tone. "This is Nemain's way of keeping track of your debts."

Those swirls solidified into black ink tentacles wrapping around his neck as if to squeeze the life from him. Finally, James lowered his hand, the pain subsiding.

Ashby crouched at his side. "What have you done?"

CHAPTER 22

LEAVE HER, JOSEPH

Joseph listened as James had announced that the pirates would no longer be a problem, earning relieved breaths and gratitude from the remaining villagers.

Once silver glistening sails could be spotted, Darla had pulled Angelica into the nearest home, arm wrapped close to her chest. She said something along the lines of Angelica still being dressed like a heathen. Although he wasn't complaining about the corset and trousers he'd come to know her in, he had to admit that would not go smoothly for her if the Commodore saw.

Roger walked up to them, a smile on his face before it dropped. He stared at James with scrutiny, no doubt seeing the fresh ink wrapped around his neck. Perhaps the bloodied hand as well.

"What happened?"

"Pike and his crew are dead, that's all you need to know," Ashby responded. Joseph noted how easily the officer defended James, even if he didn't agree with him.

Roger nodded. "Aye. I'll take it." He drowned the both of them with a suffocating hug. One he dragged Joseph into as well, patting him firmly on the back. "You've saved us and for that, we'd be holdin' you to a feast."

Ashby pulled away. "No need. The Navy will be upon us within the hour. I imagine they wouldn't want to delay our journey back."

"That may be, but all three of ya be welcome back for it. We'll be waitin' to celebrate." Roger's eyes flicked back behind Joseph. "Oh, and might I say, ya be havin' a better reason to return to our shores."

Roger's hand gripped Joseph's shoulder, effectively turning him around until he spotted Angelica leaving the hut with Darla. The corset was gone, replaced by a soft white shirt that hung loosely on her chest. The trousers were replaced by a bright orange skirt, the color making her skin glow in the new morning light. Her hair lay undone around her shoulders, much curlier than he thought it was. He wanted to touch it and feel if the strands were as soft as they looked.

"She protected my Darla when she needn't. For that, she be havin' a place among us." Roger gave him a slight push in her direction. "Now, go get ya lass." His bellowing laughter faded unto the background as he backed away, but Joseph was unwilling to take his eyes off the angel before him.

Angelica breezed towards him, a softness to her eyes he'd never seen before. How could a woman he had known a few days have such an effect on him? She was little more than a stranger, and yet, he never wanted anything more.

James beat him to it, blocking his sight with a mischievous smirk over his shoulder.

"You look ravishing," James said, his voice finding a sultrier tone. "I have to thank you for saving me when I took the book initially. I know you saw me." Her cheeks darkened as he grabbed her hand to kiss the back of it. "The name's James. I never did catch yours."

Joseph growled, the sound low and animalistic. He'd never made a sound like it before, but his jealousy threatened to spill over as he stood a step behind James.

Angelica's gaze returned to him, witnessing his lack of control, a small smile lifting the corner of her mouth. What was going on in that pretty head of hers?

"I didn't tell you." She passed by James without another glance, focusing on Joseph instead. Suddenly, he was inadequate. His hair was too messy. His clothes were too battered. Even his soul would not be worthy of this woman. The woman who defied her own father to save the island.

James nodded, accepting the defeat and leaving them be, a smile playing on his lips.

Angelica tipped her head and walked along another path. He followed like a moth to a flame, finding her beyond the village in a sunny spot among the trees. She was focused on something before her, then she turned around.

The sunlight hit her face in a way that made her skin glow.

"It's yours."

He finally focused on the object before him. In her hands was a sword, the most beautiful one he had ever seen. His father's cutlass.

"I can't say I regret stealing it." The sentiments made him laugh. Here she was, as perfect as she was, giving him the thing he once thought was his most precious possession. Now, he couldn't care less for it. "Because it led you to me. Or me to you. In whatever ways Davina works." She presented it to him. "But I wanted to give it back to you, as a thank you for saving me. In so many different ways, but mostly–" she paused, her throat working. She was so Davina-damned beautiful. "For not being a selfish bastard."

"I'm not so sure about that." Looking at her now, he felt very selfish.

Finally, he was close enough for her to pass the sword to him, one last assurance on her lips. "But you are. You could've left me to die. You could've used me to get the sword—"

His lips collided with hers, the sword tossed to the jungle floor like it was nothing but a stick. She leaned into him, her hands smoothing over his lapels as his arms encompassed her waist. He pulled her in, feeling her body against his. Everything about her was perfect, but especially the way they felt so incredibly right against each other.

Angelica sunk into him as he lifted one hand to her glorious curls. They were even softer than he thought was possible and she moaned into his mouth when he tugged on them.

"Where's my men?" The Commodore's voice was distant, but not distant enough. "I don't intend to linger."

Joseph groaned, tucking his head into her shoulder.

She laughed softly and it was the most beautiful sound he'd ever heard. "It seems you are due to board, sailor."

"That's the last thing I want to do."

Angelica smiled at him before pulling back. She fixed his hair and his uniform until it looked somewhat presentable. "You have to go; we both know that. But I'll be waiting here for your return." He watched her eyes darken and wished that he didn't have to leave her.

Their foreheads came together as he took in the rich scent of her. She smelled like sea salt, water lilies, and– apples? He smiled at the idea of that.

"Earhart! Officer, your presence is required!"

He blocked out the noise for a second longer. "I'll do whatever I must to see you again."

"I'm looking forward to it, *officer*."

"Earhart!"

He broke away from her and it felt like cleaving his soul in two.

"You left the sword."

He looked back once more. "Keep it safe for me. Maybe one day I'll need it."

The trip back to Samsara felt more like leaving home than the trip to Kheli had. Without Angelica there, Samsara wasn't home. That was a scary thought, yet he didn't hold onto fear. It felt like his life was finally beginning.

James had hidden the book in the ship's cargo compartment. He had to find a safe place to hide it where no one would find it. All three of them had an unspoken agreement never to speak of it again.

Trouble is, things that are powerful have a way of finding the wrong hands, but destroying it was no longer an option. James was tied to it. The new tattoo on his neck was evidence of that. The Commodore hadn't said a word about the breach of uniform. Something about that didn't sit right with Joseph.

They were about to land, watching the shore approach when Joseph leaned in to whisper.

"What did you mean, when you said it was too late?"

He needed to know. A guilt weighed on him that James had traded his soul in exchange for Angelica's safety.

"That might be a tale for a different day, mate. Just know I've been paying my debt to Nemain long before I came across that book."

Joseph nodded, but didn't like the sound of that. He didn't press for more though. If the right time came, James would tell him. He had faith in that.

Though there was a less burning question in his mind. "And Robin?"

A smirk resonating pride lifted his lips. "I knew you'd be smart enough to figure it out."

Joseph knew better than to speak the words aloud on *Davina's Will*. The monkey was a witch's son. The same as Pike, the very reason he was in the hairy cage. A mother's love binding him to the body of a monkey. Joseph's heart sank at the boy's fate. Would he die in that vessel as well?

James rolled up the sleeve of his arm, flashing another tattoo on his forearm, Joseph instinctively moved to shelter the view of it from the rest of the officers. The swirling pattern was smaller, the pattern resembling a monkey in some parts and a boy in others. Its face looked entirely human, but it still possessed a tail and most of its fur.

The sleeve was rolling down as a crew member passed them by. James whispered, "He's fully human now, but it will be some time before he understands how to be a boy again."

Joseph smiled thinking of the monkey that helped him save Angelica's life. "I look forward to a proper introduction."

James reflected the smile until it dropped. "You didn't find the sword, but you did find a woman in this adventure. That's something to celebrate." Joseph nodded, keeping the location of the sword to himself for the moment. He liked the idea of a secret shared with Angelica alone.

He reached out a hand, gripping James by the shoulder. "Perhaps there's a lady out there waiting for you to find her."

James leaned against the ship railing as it docked. He laughed, but the smile didn't reach his eyes. "Slim chance I'm afraid, mate. I've met all the women on this island. I wouldn't equate my happiness to any one of them."

"Don't write Davina off just yet. Fate will find you eventually."

People shouted as the ramp was released and the officers departed.

"At least in this, we can agree."

The Commodore strode up to James. "Thank you for alerting the Minister to such a precious find. I'll be sure to give him your regards." James' brows twisted as a group of men carried away a bag in the shape of a large book.

James reached for it, but Ashby was there to hold him back before the Commodore could see.

"And do be careful in the future, Hawkins. By the looks of it, that book has already corrupted you." The Commodore held a self-satisfied smile, directing his steps to the ramp, no doubt looking forward to the heavy reward such a prize would bring him.

"You? You did this?" James whispered, staring at his friend and comrade, betrayal lining his eyes.

Ashby let out a long-suffering breath. "I had to. The Minister will keep it concealed and it won't eat away at you. Maybe we can still reverse it."

James brushed him off. "The Minister is precisely the character we needed to keep that power away from," he whisper-shouted.

"There it is. Power. That's all you see it as. Not as dangerous."

James growled. "It's both! That's why we can't trust it with anyone else."

Ashby straightened, looking down on James. "I can't destroy it anymore. This was the next best thing."

"And it being in my charge is worse?"

"Yes."

James drew back like the word was a physical blow. He turned to walk away.

"James, wait."

James rushed off down the ramp, out of formation, but no one bothered to correct him.

Joseph caught the look on the Commodore's face. He watched that whole exchange from the gangplank; a winning grin on his face.

"What have you done?"

Finally, Ashby paled.

Acknowledgments

Thank you to all the support I had during this process.

To my editor, who was honest enough with me to tell me how horrible my first draft was and helped me to remake it into what it is today. Your excitement at each twist and turn has made me believe in my writing.

To Ana, for finding me in a random coffee shop and adopting me. I couldn't have asked for a better writing buddy and hype woman. I hope the world gets to see what you've created soon.

To my husband, for taking care of the house and my need to consume food while in the harrowing process of publishing. Your support means the world.

And finally, to all the readers who have made me one of their favorites. I see you cheering me on from the stands. I appreciate EVERY WORD of support I see from you guys. :)

ALSO BY MCKENZIE A HATTON

The Captain of Nemain's Revenge

The Siren of Samsara

The First Mate of Nemain's Revenge - Prequel Novella

The Demons of Draiocht (Coming 2024)

About the Author

McKenzie A Hatton's ideal night is a glass of wine and a good book. She grew up in the rolling hills of Oregon, spending time with family at the beach, and petting every animal who would let her.

McKenzie is a world traveler with a town in Ireland, Killarney, being her favorite. She is lucky to have the chance to travel and to write, the two things that make up her passions.